TWISTED FATE

TWISTED INTENTION
BOOK THREE

SUMMER COOPER

LOVY BOOKS

Lovy Books Ltd
20-22 Wenlock Road
London N1 7GU

Cover by SC Creative

1

Keily

"It's been three months since he walked out, Rosa, I don't think there's any hope," Keily spoke out loud, knowing the hands-free feature in the car would pick up what she said. She was on her way to work and not looking forward to it.

"Don't you think you should at least tell him about the babies?" Rosa asked from the car's speakers, which made Keily frown.

She hadn't known she was pregnant that night when he left her with a cruel goodbye, but she did now. Oh, she definitely knew she was now. A trip to the pharmacist for a pregnancy test proved it. Her family doctor confirmed it with a test of her own and had sent her to an OB/GYN. That doctor had another surprise in store for her, she was carrying more than one baby!

"Yeah, I probably should tell him about the babies, but, well, there's things you don't know, Rosa." Keily's voice trailed off as she pulled into the parking lot of the diner where she'd managed to wrangle a job. It wasn't her first choice, but she needed to keep busy, save money, and try not to think about Logan too much.

Eugene. Whatever his name was.

"You keep saying that, but you haven't told me what those things are so it's not like I'd know now, would I?" Rosa was getting exasperated with her, but it *was* the end of the day for Rosa. Her patience was worn thin after a day of directing human resources at Logan's South Carolina branch of his manufacturing business.

It was only the beginning of the day for Keily.

She was part-time at the diner and the owner liked to give her odd hours for not letting him know she was pregnant when he'd hired her two months ago. Her shift today would be 5-10. The day before it was 2-7. The erratic schedule really messed with her sleep cycle, especially when she was four months pregnant with triplets.

She'd learned that whopper of a surprise at her first ultrasound appointment. An appointment that was scheduled early because she was showing signs of a multiple pregnancy. The doctor suspected she'd heard three heartbeats and Keily was showing already. Add that to the extreme exhaustion that revealed itself by the dark circles under her eyes, and the overwhelming nausea that plagued her through the night, and there was enough reason to suspect she was carrying more than one baby.

She'd been delighted at the thought of twins, but triplets were a little scary. Especially when the father wasn't involved. And didn't know about the babies at all. She'd made Rosa swear not to tell him and avoided all of the places she knew he frequented. Even if Rosa said he was out in California, working on getting his business over there back up and running since the earthquake took his building down.

Avoiding him wasn't hard to do when he was out of the state and she'd moved out of the apartment he'd provided her with when he hired her as his personal assistant.

Sunlight glanced off the glass that made up most of the diner's walls and blinded Keily as she turned the engine off but left the key in the position to leave the electronics working. She still had five minutes before she had to go in and the ever-present weariness that she couldn't shake made her legs feel heavy and her head hurt. Her stomach even flipped in annoyance as a waft of oily, fried food drifted in through the vents in the car.

"Keily? Did I lose you?" Rosa's voice brought Keily out of her stupor.

"I'm still here. I've just pulled in at work. As far as Logan goes, there are personal things that I can't share with you. They aren't my secrets to tell." She paused when a pang of guilt reminded her that his secrets were also hers. Although, this secret was something she'd made herself forget, not think about, and try to ignore since that day so long ago. It was a shameful secret, one that made her feel incredibly…bad.

"I understand, then. Still, I wish I could help you fix all of this. Maybe even find you a better job." Rosa trailed off, probably thinking the same thing Keily was.

Nobody wanted to hire a pregnant lady.

"It'll be alright, Rosa. I have you and that's all I need for now." Keily was too tired to even think, but if she quit this job, she'd blow through the money she'd made from selling some of Logan's gifts to her in no time. She'd also be stuck at home with nothing but homework, and her thoughts, to keep her company.

"I hope so, honey. I'll let you go. Have a good shift." Rosa's voice picked up a little and Keily knew it was forced cheerfulness.

"Thanks, I hope you have a good night, Rosa. I'll talk to you tomorrow, okay?"

"You bet, sweetie. 'Bye." Rosa broke the connection before Keily could, which left Keily sitting in her car, staring out at the diner as the day continued its track into night.

Hungry diners would soon show up, filling the booths inside, rushing Keily off her feet as she forced a smile she'd stopped feeling a hundred smiles earlier. This working business was hard to do, working while she was pregnant was even worse. She'd do it though, as long as she could.

She had no other choice, not when she was on her own now. With a tired groan, she pushed out of the car and walked to the back door. A smiling face greeted her when the door opened to her knock. "Hi, Keily, glad you made it."

"I'm glad too, Lisa, how are you?"

"Good, just tired. It's been a long day. How are those kiddos?" Lisa shut the door as Keily walked in, her black slacks and white blouse the accepted uniform for everyone that worked at the diner. At least they didn't make her wear a stupid outfit with skirts.

"They're making their mom cranky, but they're good." Keily smiled, put her handbag in a locker, slid her phone into the black polyester blend apron tied loosely around her waist, and made sure her hair was still tied up in a neat bun.

"And how's the schoolwork?" Lisa rattled off the same questions every time she saw Keily, but Keily didn't mind. At least someone besides Rosa asked.

"It's good too, I'm struggling to get it all done, but I am," Keily answered, sugarcoating just how far behind she was. She didn't want pity, but a kind word here and there was nice.

"Good, I've got a table to get back to, but I'll see you on the floor."

"Sure, be right there." Keily paused to clock in as Lisa walked out of the area designated as the office and stared out of the little window in the swinging door. Lisa's table was the only one with customers so far. Keily had time to get prepped for the evening then. She'd be there until the place closed at 10 pm, and a little later cleaning up, but she had work to do first.

She checked to see how many salads were in the cooler, how many slices of the 'homemade' pie they sold but really bought from a mass producer were left, and made a fresh pot of coffee. Their clientele tended to be on the older side and plain coffee was what they wanted. Coffee chains might have the younger generation suckered in but the older one just preferred plain coffee, without sprinkles, whipped cream, or cinnamon.

"Hi, Mark, how are you?"

"I'm good, Keily. Burned myself on the grill earlier, but I'm okay." Mark held up his thick forearm to show her a wide bandage at the midpoint between his wrist and his elbow.

"You're more of a klutz than I am." She laughed good-naturedly and he smiled. He was a fluffy pillow of a man, as tall as he was wide and obviously loved to eat, with black hair and smiling brown eyes.

"My wife tells me that all the time," Mark answered with a rueful nod. "You're both right.

Mark was the cook for the evening shift and had been with the place since he was 18 years old. He was 38 now and still there. Lisa, on the other hand, had only started there a couple of years before Keily came along, but they were the same age. Lisa had moved to town with her husband when his father became too disabled to take care of himself. Her job at the diner was a break from her life at home and some much-needed extra income.

Both were nice and much easier to deal with than the owner. "Thad gone for the day?" Keily asked as Lisa walked up to her and Mark. She asked it as nonchalantly as she could but from Lisa's smile, Keily knew it was obvious she didn't want to see the guy. He wasn't her favorite person on good days. She couldn't handle the thought that he might come back in tonight. He did sometimes, just to keep an eye on them, she knew.

"No, he's decided to annoy his kids and take them to see that new animated film. The one about the dogs." Mark rolled his eyes as he spoke.

Thad's kids were 17 and 18 years old. They didn't want to be seen in a theater watching a kid's film, not at that age.

"You know he just wants to see it himself; those kids of his will die if he makes them see it with him." Lisa chimed in and Keily smiled in agreement.

"Oh, it's definitely him." Keily agreed, ready to talk about anything that would keep her mind off of Logan but she had to pick up an order pad and call out a greeting as a group of five came in and headed for one of the booths in her section.

The rest of her evening went by in a rush and before long, Keily was back at the trailer she now called home, staring at a secondhand television she'd bought from a group on Facebook. It was an older television, but she could watch Netflix with the help of an Android box, at least.

A quick shower when she got home, a change of clothes, and she was now on the couch that came with the trailer, covered by one of the blankets she'd bought when she was with Logan. She hadn't wanted to move into a trailer, she'd have preferred an apartment, but they were out of her price range and she had no credit since everything had either been in Joe's name or Logan's. She couldn't get into a nice, safe apartment even if she wanted to spend the money.

The trailer was tucked between two others and both her neighbors were sweet elderly ladies. The dark blue trailer behind her belonged to Mildred. It was a newer trailer and had better appliances than Keily's had. Sally lived ahead of her in a white doublewide that was roomy and comfy. Keily's, in the middle, was light brown, probably a product of the 80s, but enough for her. It had two bedrooms, two bathrooms, and came with a dishwasher. There was no pool or gym, but she was within walking distance of her employer, if it came down to that.

When she'd first realized Logan wasn't coming back, she sold some of the earrings and a watch he'd given her. That brought in a good chunk of change, it was quality stuff, and she found the best price for it that she could, but she had to be careful. She had three babies on the way and that was going to get expensive fast.

At least Logan had kept her insurance paid up, thankfully. That was a saving grace, her insurance card worked every time she used it, and lately, she'd used it a lot. Keily glanced down at the ultrasound scans on the coffee table where she'd left them. Her babies.

All three of them.

A smile replaced the grim sadness on her face. Life wasn't so bad, knowing she had them on the way. She'd like to have her sister and parents by her side, but she'd burned those bridges, well, her mom had as far as her parents were concerned. Violet was justified in ignoring Keily's attempts at reconciliation. Keily had been a selfish bitch when she was living at her sister's and didn't blame Violet a bit for walking away.

If only Logan hadn't walked away too.

Keily looked around her living room with its brown carpet and brown wallpapered walls. It was like a brown coffin. Keily thought bringing some of her stuff from the apartment would cheer the place up, but it only made it more hideous somehow. At least it was warm and dry though.

The kitchen had white appliances and was decorated with a cows and chickens theme, even the wallpaper sported the creatures. The floor in there was linoleum meant to look like pine slats, but it cleaned easily at least. The master bedroom was a garish yellow, as was the master bath, even the bathtub, while the other bedroom was a neutral olive green. At least the guest bath was plain white.

The things she'd brought looked odd in the old place and might make someone wonder if the items were stolen, but Keily needed everything she'd brought. She'd sold some of the things for a good price, but most of them she'd kept. The most expensive gifts Logan gave her, things like jewelry, were all in a safe deposit box at the bank. She wasn't naïve enough to keep those here at the trailer.

"Oh, how the mighty have fallen, babies," Keily murmured and cradled her slight bump at the same time. "Once upon a time, Mommy had a husband, a house, and everything she thought she wanted. Now, all she has is a savings account with a little bit of money in it, a car that isn't really hers, some jewelry your daddy gave her, and she lives in a trailer. But she has you and that might just be everything she needs."

A wave of nausea rolled over her in the dark room, lit only by the TV. "And I think you all hate me."

She groaned and pushed up from the couch to go to bed. Most nights, if she got to sleep before the nausea turned into vomiting, she could sleep through the night. But, if she waited too long, she'd be up for hours in the bathroom, wishing it was all over and done with.

At four months she was over a third of the way through to having her babies, but it still seemed like a long time away when everything ached and she was sick all the time. On some of the worst nights, she'd cry and wish Logan were with her, but only on those nights. Other nights she planned the babies' bedroom, trying to come up with a plan to situate three cribs in the tiny room. There'd need to be a dresser too, a changing table, a rocker.

In the back of her mind was the reminder of what the doctor said, triplets made her high risk, and there was a higher risk of complications for the babies too. She'd have to be careful and not get her hopes up too high that this would be smooth and painless. She'd learned her lesson about that already, hadn't she?

Her heart was broken, it was definitely broken, but

she couldn't call Logan or ask for his help with the babies. He'd think she got pregnant on purpose, to trap him. And after what she did, after what Joe did, she couldn't face him. Not knowing who he was. Not knowing that she'd walked away all those years ago, hadn't stopped what had happened. Instead, she'd turned her back on him and made herself forget that she'd watched Joe assault and mutilate Logan's butt cheek with her keychain. She couldn't bear to look him in the eye again, not even when she needed him the most. Not even if it was the one thing in the world she wanted most, besides for her babies to be healthy. She'd just have to get on with life, without him. Somehow.

2

Logan

Stupid. So stupid.

Logan glared at the road ahead, his thoughts, as always, on Keily. Leaving her all those months ago had been a stupid mistake. His heart tried to tell him, even one half of his brain had balked at what the other half wanted to do, but he hadn't listened. Now, he was miserable, and it was his own fault.

He'd used logic and his intelligence to guide him throughout his life. He hadn't allowed teenaged romantic entanglements to ruin his high school career. When he'd graduated to the university level, he'd enjoyed sex, but he hadn't allowed himself to become distracted by it. Later, when he'd started to make a name for himself, women were available, but he'd always held back his emotions. That hadn't been a hard thing to do.

Not until Keily came back into his life. He'd had a crush on her when he was a kid. She'd been sweet, charming, and always ready for life until puberty took over all of the kids their age. He couldn't shake that crush, maybe because he remembered that innocent charm she'd had, even when she'd learned to make snide comments and to put her nose in the air.

Logan wasn't stupid, he'd known back then he'd never stand a chance with a girl like her. There was no way he could compete with guys like Joe and his friends. Besides, being a loner meant he didn't have friends anyway. He could have dated some of the girls at school, there'd been pretty girls that were more suited to his personality, but he'd just…shut all of that down.

When she walked into his office that day, all airs and lies, he knew he should have told her who he was, should have told her he knew her resume was a lie, but he'd wanted something like revenge. Sure, living well was the best revenge but there was a part of him that wanted her to beg to have him. And she had, hundreds of times, in so many pretty, delightful ways.

That last night was a mistake though and he knew it before he'd even put his key in the ignition of his car so he could drive away. Pride wouldn't let him go back in and apologize to her. His pride wanted to enjoy that stricken look on her face, the heartbreak he'd seen in her beautifully shattered gray eyes.

Unfortunately, his heart was just as shattered as hers was.

Seeing the dawning realization on her face hadn't felt as good as he'd thought it would. Knowing he'd finally got some vengeance for that night didn't help either. Instead, that part of his brain that wanted her, needed her, told him that Keily was a young woman who had no idea how to fend off young men like Joe and his friends, that she couldn't do anything to protect herself if they turned on her. The mean streak in those guys could have easily turned to her and if they'd hurt her it would have broken Logan even more.

It was too late to realize all of that now. She probably hated him, probably didn't want to see him ever again. He had to assume she was disgusted, having begged him for sex not knowing that he was the loser she'd known as Eugene. Humiliation made people do strange things and when he figured out she'd left the apartment, on a secret drive-by late one night a week after he'd revealed who he was, he knew she must be humiliated.

The apartment was dark, and her car was gone so he'd let himself in. She'd taken most of the things she'd bought, but there was enough left behind that he knew she'd lived there. The bedroom still smelled of her perfume, the bathroom smelled of her shampoo. The only communication he'd had from her was a parcel, delivered with a whole lot of insurance attached, that contained the butterfly necklace he'd given her.

That was when he really knew he'd fucked up. He hadn't bought the necklace to goad her, or as some subliminal reminder of who he was, he'd bought it because it made him think of her. She'd always loved butterflies, even when they were kids, and he'd noticed she still did the first time he walked into her apartment. Even her screensaver at the office had been of butterflies.

His new PA changed it to sensible lines scrolling across the screen and bouncing around. He'd missed those butterflies when she quit working for him. That was probably what prompted him to buy the damn thing in the first place, his new PA's awful, boring, colored lines.

The necklace was in the safe at his house now, which was being guarded by a live-in housekeeper named Judith that he'd hired to not only keep the place clean, but also occupied while he was out in California. He had a business to rebuild from the ground up, which meant he was gone from the house in South Carolina often.

Over the last few months since the devastating earthquake that toppled his building, he'd moved his manufacturing process to a rented building and set up his offices there. It was going to cost a fortune to rebuild the old building and by the time the insurance paid out, he might be better off just buying a new place. But, he thought, as he stared through the windshield at the evening traffic that slowed his progress back to his apartment, maybe it would pay off down the road.

It wasn't a decision he had to make quickly, but he had already started the process of clearing the land of rubble and making sure health hazards were handled. He followed the law, as he should. Dividing his time between three locations left him exhausted, but usually too tired to think about Keily too much. She was always in the back of his mind, but being stuck in traffic, or in a line at the grocery store, or at home waiting on food to be delivered, or any other time when he couldn't distract himself, she was front and center in his thoughts.

"Damn" He muttered and poked at the console of his car, looking for someone, anyone to call to distract himself.

He scrolled all the way to the bottom of his list, which was Wally, his right-hand man in California. Wally had been shaken up by being buried alive, and Logan couldn't blame him. Logan let all the staff that had been trapped in the collapsed building take a couple of weeks off, with paid leave, to recuperate and destress. Wally had come back to work with less fear on his face, but there was still something haunted in his eyes.

Logan had a feeling it would be a long time before that look left Wally's eyes.

From his own traumatic experiences, Logan knew that day wouldn't be forgotten by Wally, and that it would probably haunt him for decades to come. He felt for the guy, he really did. As he did for all of his employees, but Wally was the one he was closest to out of them all.

Well, besides Keily, but she wasn't his employee anymore or his girlfriend. Lover. Whatever it was she'd been. He'd never been able to define what she was to him but that was mainly because he hadn't wanted to.

Logan finally found a name he felt like talking to and hit dial.

"Hello?" The feminine voice asked, a hint of hesitance and confusion.

"Hey, Rosa, it's me, Logan. How's things in South Carolina?" He tried to sound casual, like he was just checking up on his business, but even he could hear the falseness of that casualness.

"Um, fine, Logan. No problems. Why? What's up?" She was always a nice lady, good at her job, and a good friend to Keily and he hoped she might mention her friend now but the tenseness in her voice said that wasn't about to happen.

"Nothing, just checking to make sure all is well. I get the reports every day and they tell me the manufacturing part is fine, but I just wanted to touch base with you, find out how it's all going with the employees? Everything alright?"

"Everything is fine, Logan. No problems that all of us here can't handle." She still sounded confused and tense, perhaps even a little defensive.

He shouldn't have called her.

"Great, thanks then. I won't keep you." He rushed the words out and reached out for the button on his steering wheel that would end the call.

"You wanted to know about Keily, didn't you?"

That stopped him.

"No, she's gone and…" He couldn't think of a lie and his voice trailed off.

"She's fine. She has a job, she's got a place to live, and she's fine." Rosa's words came out slowly, guarded, and he knew she didn't want to reveal too much to him, but she did want to relay some information.

"That's, well, that's good then, I guess." He replied simply, not satisfied really, but what else could he say? Demand Rosa give him the details of Keily's life over the last few months? Demand a report with pictures, graphs, and receipts?

That wouldn't happen. First, because she wouldn't do it, and second because he wouldn't stoop to it. Keily wanted to be left alone, so he'd leave her alone.

"I guess so, Logan. Listen, I have some work to do so

I have to go. Unless there was something else you needed from me?" Her voice wasn't curt now, it was more resigned to the situation.

He could almost picture the look on her face as she spoke and he hated to be the cause of it. Rosa was nice, as an employee and as Keily's friend. She was loyal to Logan at work but loyal to Keily as a friend. He could respect that.

"No, but thanks, Rosa. Take care and I hope to be on that side of the country soon."

"I'm sure everyone will be glad to see you back over here. At work." That last part was an addition that he took to mean he should stay away from Keily.

But maybe he was reading more into it than he should. "Alright, take care, Rosa. See you soon."

"Take care, Logan. 'Bye."

The connection broke and the car filled with the sound of nothing. Logan clicked a control on the steering wheel until *Strawberry Fields Forever* by The Beatles came on to chase the silence away. Everything was great for a few minutes as he tried to figure out what kind of drugs the Fab Four must have been taking to write such weird lyrics. His moment of peace was shattered when John Lennon began to sing *Love*, however.

He almost flicked to the next track, but for the first

time in his life, he actually stopped to really listen to the song. It nearly broke him.

John Lennon might have been gone from this world for a very long time, but the words he sang so simply described exactly what Logan had never known. What love was. If he hadn't been hemmed in by other cars, he'd have pulled off the road to collect himself. Since he was stuck, he just hit replay and let the words wash over him.

Images, memories, flashed through his mind as the song played, Keily's smile, her face as he made love to her, the way she'd loved nothing more than snuggling on the couch with him, the way he made her sigh, the way she made him…feel. Fuck, this was getting out of hand, he thought, as a horn blew behind him. Traffic was moving at last and he was holding it up.

Maybe it was time to go home? Perhaps if he saw her, even a glimpse of her, he could ease this ache that felt as though it would tear his heart in two.

But he knew that was another stupid idea. The minute he saw her he'd want to talk to her, touch her, apologize for the cruelty he'd inflicted on her. What must she think of him?

He'd kept his identity a secret, misled her about so many things, and played her for a fool, whether he'd actually meant to or not. Although, he had to be honest, at first, he had wanted to mislead her, he'd wanted to hurt her the way he'd been hurt all those years ago. The more he'd come to know her, though, the less he wanted that revenge, the less he wanted to see her broken.

So why had he done it then?

He still couldn't fully explain the cognitive dissonance he'd felt the last night he was with her. He didn't want her pain anymore, he wanted to make her smile again, but he was fairly certain that ship had sailed.

The Keily he'd met all those months ago wasn't the woman he'd left that night. That original Keily, she was a schemer, out for whatever she could get. She'd changed somewhere along the way. Logan didn't know if it was his doing, or Rosa's, maybe both? Or perhaps Keily had finally been allowed the freedom to grow up, so she had?

It could have been all of those factors, but he'd never know for sure because he'd blown his own chance at happiness for a moment of petty revenge. And the fucking nightmares hadn't stopped either. It seemed they never would.

3

Keily

"How long have you got left on your shift?" Rosa asked from the opposite side of the booth she and Keily occupied.

"A few hours," Keily said with a complete lack of enthusiasm. Another month had passed, her bump had grown at least another inch, or so her pants told her, but little else had changed. "I just want to go home."

"So why don't you just quit, Keily?" Rosa was a little exasperated with her, but sighed before she went on, her face downcast. "I'm sorry, Keily. I didn't mean to be so harsh."

"I know," Keily said, reaching across the table for her friend's hand. "I just don't want to spend what I have saved up. I'm getting through school alright, and when I'm done with that, I might take a break, or find a less demanding job with the degree, but right now, I want to save that nest egg for my maternity leave and any future problems I might need to spend my way out of."

"I guess that makes sense. Although..." She paused as if to consider what she was about to say, her left eyebrow, dark and perfectly shaped, arched over her brown eye "If you told Logan about the babies, he'd probably help you out. The state may insist he pay child support anyway."

"If I put him on their birth certificates," Keily answered promptly, feeling the sting of truth in Rosa's words. "Life would be simpler, I know, if I just told Logan but you know what he'll say. First, he'll ask if they're his, then he'll think I did it on purpose."

"You do know it takes two to make babies, right?" Rosa asked with a soft laugh, to take the snark out of what she'd said.

"I do." Keily laughed in return, her gray eyes wide with delight. "I know that too well. But you know how men can be, it's always our fault if we get pregnant, our fault they didn't wear a condom when they should, our fault we didn't do...something."

"I'm not sure Logan is that kind of guy. He's so... caring sometimes. Like all the people in California that work for him, he gave them weeks off with pay, has made sure his worker's comp insurance company doesn't stiff any of them, and he's always checking on everyone, even while he's been in California. He still calls me, the other supervisors, even the employees that got friendly with him. He takes care of his people. I'm not so sure he'd blame you for those little wiggle worms in your tummy."

"Wiggle worms, fuck, don't say that. I'll have nightmares about it when I can actually get some sleep." Keily looked around, even though the diner was empty. She wanted to be sure someone hadn't sneaked in without her noticing. With a sigh she let Rosa's hand go and leaned back in the booth.

Lisa was around somewhere, probably preparing hash-browns for the cook or sweeping somewhere. She was always busy and even did some of the chores Keily was supposed to do because she didn't want Keily doing them. Especially the mopping. She was terrified Keily would slip and it would hurt the babies, so she wouldn't let Keily anywhere near a wet floor.

It was kind of her, but Keily felt a little bit like she was taking advantage of the older woman, even if she did insist on doing it.

"That new smock, ahem, suits you." Rosa pointed at the white shirt with light pink stripes.

The top of the smock was too big, but her breasts were ballooning so she'd gone two sizes too big when she bought it. There were pleats gathered just below her bustline that would accommodate her stomach as it grew. Not her idea of high fashion, but she had a limited choice when it came to work clothes. The pink stripes were pushing it, but they were very light so hopefully, they wouldn't get her in trouble with the boss.

"I think it looks like I'm wearing a tent, but what can you do?" Keily shrugged and smiled, brushing her hand over her blonde hair to make sure it was still in a neat bun. "I even had to buy maternity pants."

"Oh no, are they awful to wear?" Rosa cringed and looked down at Keily's waist, even though the table covered most of it.

"They aren't bad really, that stretchy part even helps my back a little. And I found this support thing that cradles the bump too, that's a big help." Keily's hand came down from her hair and settled on her ever-expanding stomach. A smile twitched at her lips and she sighed with something like happiness. "I know I'm always talking about how miserable this is, but it's nice too, you know?"

"No, I don't," Rosa said, her brown eyes rolling in her head, but the smile downplayed it. "And I don't want to know right now."

"How's it going with your couple?" Keily slid her

glass of water over to sip at it innocently, but the grin that formed took away that innocent look.

"It's going," Rosa said primly, her eyes giving away just how pleased she was with the situation. "I'm seeing them later."

"I'm glad you're happy, Rosa." Keily meant it too. Even if she was currently miserable with her love life she was glad Rosa had found happiness. "You deserve to be happy after your divorce."

"I am. I just wish I could fix things for you." Rosa sighed again and looked away. Keily smiled at the pretty picture her friend made.

Rosa had pushed her sunglasses up on top of her head, sweeping her black hair away from her tanned face. The woman could have, should have been a model, she was so beautiful, but that wasn't the life Rosa had reached for. She'd divorced around the same time Keily had and moved into town hoping for a new direction in life, a change. She'd not only made friends with Keily, but she'd also started a romantic relationship with a married couple.

"I have to admit, at first, I kind of thought it was a crazy thing for you to do, but I wasn't judging you, by the way," Keily added quickly. "I just didn't see how it would work with a married couple. Don't you, or they, get jealous of each other?"

"No, we talk things out and treat each other with

respect. There would be issues if we were sneaking around behind each other's backs and doing things with only one but not the other. We communicate and that's important in all relationships."

"You're right." Keily nodded, knowing that was one thing that was really lacking when she'd been with Logan. Oh, they'd talked about things, even had some long discussions about politics, how to fix the world, other things they wanted to do or see, and a little bit about their pasts, but they'd never really talked about emotions, needs, or what might be bothering the other. It wasn't a good way to maintain a relationship, that was for sure.

Keily glanced up, about to ask Rosa something else, but she saw a woman with a baby in her arms walking up to the door. Her jaw dropped open before her entire body froze.

"What? Who is it?" Rosa asked and turned around. "Isn't that your sister?"

"It is. Shit, what do I do?" Keily glanced back at Rosa, her stiff body tense now as she leaned forward.

She'd begged her sister to talk to her, had sent her hundreds of messages, emails, and phone calls, but she'd never replied. Violet had looked Keily right in the eye as she walked in, so she knew Keily was there. She hadn't turned around and walked away, did that mean she wanted to see her sister at last? Or was she coming to gloat at Keily's fall from the top of the world?

"You should greet her and give her a menu, I guess, Keily," Rosa whispered. "Just don't be snippy. See what she does and don't let her get to you."

"You're right," Keily said quietly, lost in thought. Why was Violet really here?

"Well, go on then." Rosa hissed, her eyes wide and curious. "See what she wants. She might have gotten over it all. You won't know until you go talk to her."

"Okay," Keily whispered under her breath and pushed up from the booth. She walked over to the counter to grab a menu and a booster seat before she plastered a fake smile on her face. Violet had taken a booth by the windows at the front of the diner, further down from where Keily and Rosa sat.

"Hi, Violet, how are you today?" Keily asked in her most businesslike voice.

Her eyes were on her niece, not her sister. Alice, now two years old, had a mass of blonde curls on her head and a face that matched her mother's and Keily's. Was that what her babies would look like, Keily wondered, like miniature Alices? Her heart melted at the thought and for a moment she thought tears would overcome her, but she took a deep breath and fought them down.

"Fine, Keily. How are you?" Violet looked Keily up and down while Alice, her daughter, fidgeted in her lap.

Her eyes went wide when she noticed the smock and her eyes quickly went back up to Keily's, a question there that Keily didn't want to answer. Even if it was obvious what the answer was.

"I'm good," Keily replied, fake smile brittle as could be. How was she going to get through this?

Alice continued to fidget until Keily handed the seat over to Violet. Violet put the seat down beside her and put Alice in it before she looked back up at her older sister.

"When is the baby due?" There was no judgment there, just curiosity.

"In March," Keily answered automatically. She'd already become accustomed to people asking her that. Even the sister she hadn't seen in over a year and a half.

"I see," Violet answered, and Keily could tell she was doing the math, confused.

It was unusual that Keily had such a noticeable bump at this point in her pregnancy, but that was what happened when you were carrying around three growing humans inside of you.

"I'm going to have triplets." Keily supplied and saw understanding mixed with shocked surprise.

"You're kidding!" Violet whispered dramatically, her eyebrows high on her forehead. "Triplets?"

"Yes, triplets." Keily thawed a little as she talked about her babies and decided what to do next. "Look, I know I'm supposed to be asking you what you want to eat but it's been a long time and, well, you're here so either you want to gloat, or you want to talk. Can I sit down?"

"Sure, yeah, that's fine," Violet answered and pointed at the booth across from her.

"Alright," Keily replied and slid into the booth. "I guess since you agreed and you're here you don't want to gloat."

"No, not really. I heard around town that you were working here and about where you were living and I just wanted to check on you. I said some pretty awful things to you and then I ignored you and, wow, I still can't get over triplets. A lot has happened." Violet looked contrite and Keily felt her own guilt flare-up.

"You didn't say anything that I didn't deserve, Violet. I was awful to you, to Alice, to myself. I'm really sorry I've been such a bitch your whole life, too."

"I guess that was more Mom's doing than yours. I saw what she did to you, how she treated you, and while she thought you were some kind of precious angel, I could see she was using you. I should have understood that better." Violet smiled sadly across to her sister.

"Why should you? You were a kid and I was a monster. And yeah, Mom's to blame for a lot of that, but I made my own choices and I regret a lot of them." Keily looked away this time, her eyes full of tears she tried desperately to hold back. "A lot has changed, a lot will change again shortly, when I have these babies, but I won't ever stop feeling bad about how I treated you for far too long."

"Oh, let's just... damn it, Keily." Violet reached for a napkin and wiped at her own eyes, her eyeliner smudging as she dabbed. "I needed time to come to grips with things, but I understand now. And I'm willing to give being your sister another chance if you are?"

"I am. I really am." Keily reached to grab at Violet's hand and almost sobbed with relief when Violet grasped back.

"Oh my God, you two are going to make me cry too." Rosa sobbed from her booth and they all laughed then.

"Rosa, come meet my little sister," Keily called out before she looked back at Violet. "You'll love Rosa, she's my best friend."

"You have a best friend, Keily? You hate other women." Violet exclaimed, surprised all over again.

"I told you things have changed," Keily said with a huge smile just as Rosa came and slipped into the booth with her.

"Hi, I'm Rosa. Nice to meet you." Rosa held out her hand to Violet with a huge grin.

"I'm Violet, nice to meet you too," Violet answered and shook Rosa's hand. "And this is my daughter Alice."

"Oh, she's adorable." Rosa smiled at Alice before she

looked back at Keily. "Think your munchkins will look like her? She looks just like you and Violet."

"Probably. Although, I'm not sure the world is ready for three more of me."

"Maybe you'll have boys." Violet was quick to add. "But you aren't Mom, so maybe your kids will be, uh, different."

"Nice save, sis." Keily laughed but nodded too. "I don't think my kids will be anything like me, or well, how I was. I am most definitely not Mom."

"I know I don't know her, but from what you've told me Keily, and what Violet just implied, I don't think you'll be anything like her. Nothing at all. Besides, you'll have us to temper that snobby attitude if it comes back."

"I was never snobby to you." Keily protested immediately, her eyebrows up.

"No, but you weren't exactly Miss Congeniality at work for a while. With everyone but me."

"Yeah, you're probably right," Keily admitted. "But I just wanted to focus on doing a good job."

"Hey, you don't have to tell me, I get it. Others might have taken it for snotty superiority, but I know it was just your defense mechanism." Rosa held up her hands and leaned into Keily. "That you don't need anymore.

"No, I don't. And it seems I have my sister back at last, too." Keily smiled and looked over at her sister. "I'm so happy you stopped by."

"I am too. Now, what kind of food do they make here? I'm starving." Violet laughed as Keily handed over the menu. Keily felt herself blushing but didn't care. Something had finally gone right and nothing could take away her smile.

4

Logan

December was a shitty month as far as Logan was concerned, even during the good years. This year it was downright atrocious. Sure, things were looking up in California, the business was doing well, despite the major loss he'd suffered because of the earthquake, and he was helping his employees to stay on their feet. But, and it was a big but, December still sucked.

Mainly because he still missed that fucking woman.

Happy couples with families at their sides jostled everywhere in their best winter garb, looking like they were ready for an Instagram shoot while he was alone, miserable, and now back in South Carolina. He had a court date, one he couldn't miss, the prosecuting attorney informed him. So there he was, walking into a courthouse full of miserable people, whether they were there to work or were part of a court case. He was just waiting for this day to be over so he could get back to his house.

He wondered if he'd see Keily today, knew she'd been subpoenaed, so he likely would. His brain was split in half again, happy at the thought of seeing her and depressed because he'd see her and wouldn't be able to talk to her. Then there was the whole Joe thing. The guy who assaulted him, tore his pants off and branded his ass with a butterfly keychain, and then had the compunction to assault him again.

Logan let Joe get away with the first assault all those years ago. Not because he was afraid of the guy, or his moronic friends. No, he'd let him get away with it because all he wanted to do was get out of town and get on with the rest of his life. He'd put all of that behind him. All of it but the nightmares, that is.

They'd been even worse last night. He knew he had to get up and fly to South Carolina, and the reason why, and his brain had tortured him all night. He relived that night over and over again, until he finally jumped out of bed and gave up on sleep. Today was going to be bad, he knew it, for far too many reasons.

Logan spotted the prosecuting attorney and walked over to him. "Good morning."

"Hey, Logan, good to see you. Flight okay?" Felix asked, his eyes bright and intelligent. He was obviously a morning person. Which was probably for the best because Logan wasn't.

"Yeah, I'm good, flight was fine. Ready to get this over with." Logan grumbled, not daring to look at anyone but Felix. He didn't know when Keily would show up but if he didn't see her, he didn't have to think about her, did he?

He knew he was only delaying the inevitable, but he didn't care. He just wanted all of this to be done and over with. Maybe then the nightmares would go away too.

"Right, we're up first so let's get in there and get this started. His lawyer is out of continuances, unless something drastic has happened and from what I understand, today is the day. We'll get this done and over with for you, buddy."

"Glad to hear it," Logan muttered, head high, black wool coat buttoned up to keep the chill away. He unbuttoned the coat as he got into the courtroom and sat behind Felix on the first bench in the row behind the prosecuting attorney's table on the right.

He didn't look around, but he did rise when the judge finally came in, and sat down when so ordered. The judge droned on, a few defense attorneys had some business to attend to with him, and people came and went around his bench. Logan tuned it all out until he heard his name called. It was Felix, trying to get his attention.

"Come up here and sit with me until you're called to the stand, Logan."

Logan realized then the trial had already started, he'd just been too lost in his own world to notice. He pulled off his coat, put it on the back of the chair at the table, and sat down. The judge read over the docket and then gave the floor to the defense attorney first. Logan didn't care which of them went first, as long as it was under way, at last.

The defense attorney tried for one more continuance, but the judge wasn't having it. Logan could tell the defense attorney didn't think he'd get it, by the way he sighed and shrugged. Oh well.

Logan glanced behind him when he heard the door to the courthouse open, an automatic action, not one he'd planned at all. His eyes felt as if they would bulge out of his head when he saw who had walked in.

Keily. Beautiful, breathtaking, life-altering Keily.

Also, a very, *very* pregnant Keily.

How could she be that damn pregnant, he wondered with a frown as she found a seat and sat down, Rosa at her side. She hadn't even looked in his direction as she came in or when she found a place to sit, but he'd seen her.

"Fuck." Logan mumbled under his breath and turned back around.

"What's the matter?" Felix leaned over to whisper while Joe's lawyer called him to the stand.

"Nothing, just pay attention to that bozo," Logan whispered back, his hands clenched into fists.

Who'd gotten her pregnant, he had to wonder. Had she moved on so quickly? But when he thought about how big she was, he counted back and knew he had to be the father. It had been five months and she was much further along than that. She might even go into labor here in the courtroom by the looks of her.

Rosa was with her and sat with her now, but even she hadn't looked up at Logan when they came in. He didn't mind that Rosa was with her, he was just noting that the woman wasn't at work. He knew it was all approved somewhere along the way. Rosa was a good employee and wouldn't call in sick just to give her friend moral support. She'd put in for a day off or used a vacation day to do it.

Not that it really mattered, he thought, as Joe rambled on about his old glory days and how he'd been a hero back in the day. He then went on about how he'd been famous in the area, but a knee injury had made life hard for him. Logan couldn't help but roll his eyes as he tuned into the sob story for a moment.

Joe had always been a dick and used any excuse he

could to justify his actions. He'd become a drunk, somewhere along the way, and even that he blamed on the knee injury. Logan knew Joe was a drinker, even when they were in middle school. His addiction had nothing to do with that knee injury. Maybe shit at home or pure selfishness had led a young Joe to drink, but the adult Joe was just a major prick, looking to use his story to get out of prison. Logan had zero sympathy for him.

The attorney finished his questions and Felix stood up to ask some rather damning questions of Joe. They were quick-fire, almost staccato, and the questioning was over before Logan knew it. But the questions were significant, the answers a glaring admission of the fact that Joe had broken the conditions of his probation, and had assaulted Logan out of nothing more than jealousy. Logan knew Joe had just sent himself to prison and sat back, happy over that part, at least.

Logan waited as the police officer who'd responded to the complaint went through his testimony, his thoughts once again on Keily. Why hadn't she told him she was pregnant if they were his babies? He knew they must be, had to be, for her to be that far along.

So why the fuck hadn't she told him? he wondered angrily, his jaw clenched as tightly as his fists. Because you were a douche to her, moron, his brain told him. You humiliated her, broke her heart, and left her like a toy you were tired of playing with. Why would she have called to tell you she was pregnant when she more than likely wanted nothing to do with you?

"Damnit." He muttered again and looked off to his right. This trial was done, Joe was going to prison, and Logan was no longer interested. Joe had boldly crowed about punching Logan and said he'd do it again. Logan highly doubted any judge would let that pass him by. Especially after Joe had finished his down-on-his-luck story a few minutes before. Going from that to cocky dipshit hadn't won him any points.

"Seriously, Logan, what's up?" Felix hissed, and Logan turned to look at him.

"Keily's pregnant," Logan answered stupidly, his eyes hinting that Felix should look back at her.

"Whoa," Felix said when he glanced back at Keily. Logan could see the shock on the man's face. "That your kid?"

"Has to be for her to be that pregnant," Logan mumbled softly, his head tilted toward Felix, but his eyes straight ahead.

"You didn't know?" Felix whispered the question, his head tilted to Logan.

"Nope," Logan answered. "But that's my own fault. I'll explain later."

"Sure, Logan." Felix frowned. "If you need anything, let me know."

"I'm good, just surprised, that's all."

She'd been pregnant when he left her, she must have been. And for her to be that far along, she had to have known for a while. Why hadn't she told him then?

He thought back to those months, how happy she'd been, and how things had changed towards the end. He'd become distant, unapproachable. Some days he didn't bother to call her or text her at all. When did she have the chance to tell him?

She could have blurted it out at any point, he decided, but something like that must be a hard thing to admit when it was the two of them. She must have been walking on eggshells, trying to find the right time. Only he'd never given her that opportunity.

Either he wasn't there, came and went too fast for her to have a chance, or spent most of his time with her occupying her with other matters. Matters that had obviously created a baby.

She looked good, healthy, in a pastel yellow coat dress, those overwhelmingly sexy black heels on her feet. He still loved those shoes.

Not what he needed to be thinking about right now, he reminded himself and took a deep breath. He'd wait for the end of the trial, or a recess, one of the two, then he'd approach her and ask her why she hadn't told him.

Yeah, he knew why, but if it was his child then he had a right to know, didn't he? He wasn't the kind of monster that would disown his own child. He'd never really planned to have kids, or wanted to have them, but if that was his baby, he intended to be a part of its life. It didn't matter to him that he'd broken it off with her, that he'd been the one that dropped her like a blanket infected with smallpox, he wanted to know if that was his child.

A lump formed in his throat as he thought about a baby of his own. He didn't know that he'd feel this way, like the world had suddenly changed, just because he'd made a child with a woman. He didn't know he'd want to be a part of its life so much either. Thoughts and emotions whirled through his mind, annoying and agitating him as the minutes passed.

He'd have to talk to her somehow, find out where she lived if he had to, but one way or another, he had to talk to her. He had a right to know his child, to be a part of its life, if it was his. And there wasn't much he knew about the situation, but he did know that Keily hadn't been with anyone but him since they'd first been together. He doubted she'd been with anyone since she left Joe.

She might have taken up with someone since he left her all those months ago, but it had only been five months. She had to at least be eight months along. Of course, he was no expert on how big women got when they were pregnant, but he knew enough to know that she was really big, uncomfortably big, close to term big.

"Can you stop fidgeting, Logan? You're distracting me." Felix hissed under his breath.

"Sorry." Logan tried to focus, to bring his thoughts back to what was taking place in the courtroom. He watched Joe's attorney strut around, prodding at the cop with arrogance and a snide attitude that made Logan cringe. That wasn't helping Joe at all.

Felix asked his own polite questions before he let the cop get off the stand. Keily was next, and Logan held his breath as she got up from her seat and walked up to be sworn in. She didn't look at him, or at Joe for that matter, she looked at the bailiff and then straight at the defense attorney as he asked her a few brief questions.

Felix stood up when it was his turn to question Keily and Logan wanted to demand he ask her if that baby was his, but Felix ignored Logan's tug at his arm. Keily looked at Felix, at the judge, behind him at Rosa, but never quite at Logan or he'd have asked her with a facial expression, by mouthing the words if he had to.

"Ms. Matthews-Miller, I hate to be impolite, but I have one further question. You're divorced from Mr. Miller now, but just to clarify, is that his child you're carrying?"

"No, sir, it's not. I've not had anything to do with Joe since we divorced, except for that night he showed up at my place and assaulted Logan. This pregnancy had nothing to do with that, at all." Keily's response was prim, but not snotty. It also didn't reveal a lot to Logan. Felix had tried at least.

Damn. He'd have to corner her before she left the courthouse.

5

Keily

Logan could just fuck right off, Keily thought as she practically waddled back to her row and took a seat. She knew he'd seen her, knew he was agitated, but she didn't want to talk to him. The only reason she was there was because she had to be, she didn't want to go to jail for not showing up as directed to.

This was a nightmare for her, one she'd tried to get out of by asking to be removed from the case. The prosecuting attorney's office said she was a direct witness so she'd have to appear at the courthouse on the date given, pregnant or not. That hadn't pleased her at all.

She sat there, her ex-husband on one side, her ex-lover on the other, and relived the humiliation and heartache both had caused her over the years. Well, to be fair, Joe had caused more than his fair share for far longer than Logan had. But Logan had broken her heart more than Joe ever could because she'd actually loved him when he walked out on her.

And the babies.

Although, he hadn't known about them, so she couldn't blame him for that.

Well, he knew now, if the way he stared at her was anything to go by. She could feel his eyes on her, almost burning a hole through her, as she testified against her ex-husband on his behalf.

Not that she was angry with him, she couldn't blame him for leaving her. It was the why, why he'd called her in for a job interview in the first place that really…hurt.

Yes, she decided as Rosa stroked her left hand reassuringly, it was the fact that he'd played her, and she'd never suspected a thing that really tore a hole through her very being. She knew she deserved it though. She'd been so mean to him when they were in high school together, always saying snotty things to him just because he was there, and different, and Joe hated him for some reason. So she'd been a bitch to him, as she had been to so many other people in her life.

There was also the fact that she'd been there that night, she'd left him, and worst of all, she'd never told a soul. She stayed home for a few days after that night, afraid of Joe and his friends, but in the end, the boy that made her heart melt one day and beat with fear the next, had sweet-talked her into a night in the back of his car. She forgot that Eugene even existed, until the night he'd left her, as a man now named Logan.

Then there was Joe. He hadn't been physically abusive often, usually it was verbal and emotional pain he caused her. But there'd been times, bruises she'd become expert at hiding, and she hated seeing him again. He was also a reminder of what she used to be, who she used to be.

She wasn't that hateful, greedy person anymore, and even Violet was giving her another chance at being a sister and an aunt to Alice.

"You alright?" Rosa whispered to her, her warm brown eyes straight ahead.

"Yeah, mostly. The babies are kicking the shit out of me and I hate being here with these two, but I'll get through it. Thanks for coming." Keily leaned into her friend for support and clasped at her hand. It really was nice to have someone to lean on, emotionally and physically. Even with the bump support and the support hose she had on, her back was killing her. She knew it was only going to get worse as the babies grew, but she didn't mind too much.

"I wouldn't have let you come by yourself, you know that. I took a vacation day when you told me you had to appear despite the triplets, so I'm getting paid to be here with you. That's a good thing to me. I'll ask if you can go when they take a break." Rosa leaned her head against Keily's and they both sat quietly while the trial went on.

It was a simple enough case and should be done by the afternoon. But she wanted to go home, crawl into her bed, and watch Netflix until her eyes closed and the world faded away. Especially since she knew Logan would be on her as soon as he got the chance, to ask her about the babies.

She didn't want to talk to him about them, she decided, as she rubbed at her belly with her free hand. She wanted to ignore him for the rest of her life. He'd left her, for good reason, and she lived with the shame and humiliation of it all. Talking to him now would just add to her misery.

He would accuse her of getting pregnant on purpose, of tying herself to him in the most underhanded way a woman could. She hated that thought and didn't want him to feel obliged to come anywhere near her, or even remember that she existed. She hadn't told him for that very reason. Logan had moved on with his life, hadn't contacted her or spoken to her at all since he'd left that night.

Rosa told her he was busy in California and she hadn't doubted that he was. The earthquake had destroyed his building, so it was hardly surprising that he stayed out there. But Keily suspected that it was also because of her that he stayed away. He hadn't wanted to see her, be near her, and she couldn't blame him for that.

Guilt ate at her as the minutes passed, guilt that she hadn't taken better precautions, guilt that she'd been who she was for so long, guilt that she hadn't recognized him when she first met him. Oh yeah, there was also the guilt over the fact that when she'd first 'met' him, she'd wanted to use him for sex and whatever she could get out of him.

"I need to go to the bathroom." She whispered to Rosa suddenly, her voice tight and full of emotion.

"Want me to come with you?" Rosa turned, her eyebrows knitted with concern.

"No, stay here, I'll be fine." Keily slid to the edge of her seat and used the back of the bench in front of her to pull herself up. It wasn't easy, but she managed with the help of Rosa's hand at the small of her back.

When she finally made it to the bathroom, she inspected her image in the mirror above the sinks. The pastel yellow dress wasn't a typical winter color, but that was one of the reasons she'd liked it so much when she found it in the consignment shop. It was a bright color that had made her smile. It suited her blonde hair and light eyes and made her look less washed out.

The pregnancy was taking a toll on her body and her health. How she'd managed to get pregnant with triplets she would never know. Multiples didn't run in her family, as far as she knew. Fate must have decided she'd have all of her babies at once because she knew one thing for sure, after this pregnancy, she doubted she'd ever want to do it again. Even if Lisa told her that she would, as time passed. Lisa had never been pregnant with triplets, so what did she know?

Keily wiped at her eyeliner when she noticed some of it was smudged under her right eye, and put on more lipstick. Her bladder protested at having so much weight pressed against it and she waddled towards the first toilet. She sat there, almost at peace for a moment as she hid from the world outside the bathroom door. Logan couldn't come in here and Joe wouldn't bother if he knew what was good for him. She was safe from them both in here.

As she struggled to grab hold of her panties and pull them up, along with the support hose, she reminded herself that she was well on her way to a degree, she was supporting herself, and she'd changed over the last year and a half. She wasn't the same woman that left Joe, though she didn't regret that at all. That was probably her first step to becoming an actual human being with kindness and thoughtfulness in her heart.

"Why do they make these cubicles so fucking small?" Keily muttered as she tried to stand up without letting go of her underwear and hose. She had to turn against the cheaply painted white wall of the cubicle and push herself up because she was afraid the door wouldn't hold if she put her weight against it. Not that the flimsy privacy wall was much better, but she wouldn't have so far to fall if it collapsed under her weight.

She felt like an overinflated balloon, stretched and too big to be handled with anything but extreme care or it would pop. Tears stung at her eyes, humiliation washing over her again as she lost her grip on the hose. This really fucking sucked.

She allowed self-pity to wash over her for a moment before she lifted her head again and sighed. "There's no use in crying, girl, get your panties up and stop being a baby."

There was nobody else in the bathroom, she could talk to herself all she wanted to. She looked up at the ceiling while she got her emotions under control and saw plain tiles painted with the same cheap white paint as on the cubicle walls. The floor sported those utilitarian gray tiles that seemed to be in almost every government building she'd ever been in. For a moment, as she wiggled until the hose finally came up over her bump, she wondered if they'd started out white too and had dulled to gray over time.

"You okay in there?" Rosa called out as she walked into the bathroom.

Keily heard the door close and smiled. "Yeah, just

being your average roly-poly, trying to get her panty-hose to stay up."

"Need some help?" Rosa asked, always helpful.

"Nah, I've got it now," Keily answered as she smoothed down her dress and opened the door. "It takes getting used to, being this big."

"I can imagine," Rosa said, even though her face said she couldn't imagine how Keily was coping at all. "I think I'd go without the support hose and underwear, altogether, if I was you."

"I would if the hose didn't help ease some of the pain in my back." Keily sighed and washed her hands. "As for panties, it's just habit, isn't it?"

"I guess," Rosa answered and twisted her face around into a frown. "Logan's outside."

"I know," Keily replied, not sure why Rosa was mentioning him again.

"No, I mean outside the bathroom. He's waiting for you." Rosa said, punctuating her statement with a nod of her head towards the door.

"Shit," Keily muttered and dried her hands with the brown paper towels from the dispenser on the wall. "He's figured it out then, I guess."

"Well, he would be kind of stupid if he hadn't figured it out." Rosa laughed a little. "I mean, you look like you're about to give birth, so it has to be his, right?"

"I hadn't thought about that. He can't know it's

triplets though." Keily sank back against the wall, staring at her friend with helplessness. "What do I say?"

"Just tell him you're doing fine and don't need him. Or tell him that you're not fine, that you need help, they're his babies too and he should be here for them. Tell him what you think best, Keily. That's what you do."

Keily frowned and nodded. Rosa didn't know the whole story, so she didn't know Logan wasn't just a dick that had left her at the worst possible moment. She didn't know that Keily felt that she'd got exactly what she deserved, she just knew her friend was hurt and alone when she shouldn't be. Keily put a hand on Rosa's arm and smiled over at her. "Thanks. I'll figure it out, I guess."

"I hope so, I hate seeing you so torn up over it. I'd kick him if I could." Rosa even growled a little there at the end.

"It's not all his fault, Rosa." Keily reminded the other woman.

"I know, you keep telling me that, but I can't help how I feel."

"I know." Keily smiled to reassure her friend and nodded at the door. "You go on ahead, I'll be in when I've finished this little confrontation with Logan."

"Alright but promise me you'll just walk away and come sit with me if he's too much of a dick to you." Rosa's eyes pleaded with Keily, so she nodded again.

"I will, promise."

Rosa walked out at last and Keily took one last breath, straightened her spine as much as she could with her babies bowing her back, and tried to take a step. Fear made that impossible. Not fear of physical harm, but fear of crying in front of him, or that she'd make a fool of herself in some other way.

Yeah, she'd approached her relationship with Logan coldly in the beginning but somewhere along the way, she'd fallen in love with the broody asshole that made her smile. He'd made her cry too, she knew that, but he'd made her laugh, feel secure, cared about, and cared for. Then he left her.

That hurt, it stung worse than that time she'd gotten into a wasp nest when she was a kid, but there wasn't anything she could do to make any of it better. She'd deserved what he did to her and she couldn't change that. The only reason he was out there now, waiting to confront her, was because she was so obviously pregnant.

She hadn't thought about the fact that she'd have to go to court when he'd first left her. She'd hidden from him when Rosa let her know he was in town, but then she got the subpoena and knew he'd find out she was pregnant. There was no denying it when she was this big. She'd tried to get out of coming, but the prosecuting attorney's office wouldn't hear of it.

The moment she'd dreaded was now at hand and she had to face it.

Finally, her right foot moved, and then her left. She plastered a blank look on her face and opened the door.

"Keily." Logan started, but then stopped.

"Logan," Keily replied, her eyes open and staring right at him.

He looked so good, the same man she'd curled into so many times for comfort and love, even if they'd never said those words. He was worried, she could see that in the tension at the corners of his mouth and eyes, but still, he was just so…handsome.

"Is it mine?" He asked, interrupting her thoughts.

"Pardon?" She asked, her brows knit in confusion. Was what his? She'd been too lost in looking at him to comprehend what he'd asked.

"The baby." He answered with a slight nod to her stomach.

"Baby?" She asked in surprise. Oh, right, he didn't know. "Oh, the *babies*. There's three of them."

"Three?" His eyebrows shot up. He leaned back a little as if to get away from her.

That stung, but she hid it behind another blank look.

"Yes, three. Our triplets."

"Ours?" Logan's face went slack and he stared back at her. "Ours."

"Ours." Keily agreed, her heart thumping too fast in

her chest, stealing her breath away for a moment. This wasn't going well at all, but then she hadn't really expected it to.

"I think we need to talk then." Logan pulled his lips in, his brows drawn together again. "After court. I'll take you to dinner or whatever you want."

"Alright." What else could she do but agree?

"I'll see you then." He said before he turned and walked away.

Okay, no tears, no embarrassment, just an agreement to meet with him after court was over for the day. Good. That went better than she'd expected it to, she thought, as relief flooded through her. Now she just had to get through the conversation he wanted to have later.

6

Logan

*L*ogan somehow managed to get through the rest of the day without dragging Keily off to his car for an explanation, something he thought about over and over as the day wore on. Occasionally, he'd glance over at Joe, happy that the man looked so miserable. He went between the two of them for the rest of the day.

He hated the fact that he was enjoying someone's misery, but Joe deserved it. He deserved more, because of what he'd done to Logan when they were younger, but this would do. Then his thoughts would shift back to Keily and he had a headache by the time the judge ended court for the day.

Logan waited until Felix got up and then stood

himself.

"We'll be back here tomorrow morning at 9 am." Felix held out his hand to Logan and they shook. "I'm sorry, I've got to get home, it's my wife's birthday."

"Oh, right, yeah, have a good evening then." Logan's eyes were already searching for Keily. Her birthday was in December too, Christmas Eve.

He couldn't believe she was carrying triplets but looking at her, he guessed it was possible. She looked like she could barely stand up under the strain, but she managed it. Keily always did find a way to stay standing. She was a fighter.

"See you, Logan," Felix replied once he'd packed up everything and headed off.

Logan finally found Keily and Rosa when he went outside the courthouse. Rosa was standing protectively behind Keily, her eyes narrowed at him. He didn't know what Keily might have told the other woman but whatever it was, it looked like she wanted to chew Logan up and spit him out.

"Hi." He said gently, afraid to poke the bear.

"Hi!" Rosa and Keily said in unison.

"Um, Keily, can I take you to dinner?" He asked, looking at her to avoid the glare of Rosa's eyes.

"I, well, yes, you can." She kept her eyes on the ground as she spoke, and he wondered whether she'd bolt if he made a move towards her. Not that she'd be bolting anywhere at the moment.

"I drove her here so if you plan on taking her out you either agree to take her home or bring her back to me." Rosa ground out, her jaw clenched. Logan looked at her and saw the anger flaring in her eyes. He frowned because he knew he deserved it, but he didn't like seeing it. He liked Rosa and hated that she was mad at him.

"I'll take her home, if that's alright with you, Keily?"

"It's fine, let's just, fuck, let's just get this over with." She turned and hugged Rosa before she turned back to him, a handbag slung over her shoulder. "Let's go."

Logan nodded and put his hand at her back to guide her towards his car.

"I don't need your hand there, thank you." She moved away from him.

"Sorry, old habit." He replied and then rolled his eyes at his own stupid reminder of what he'd done. "Sorry."

"It's fine." She breathed in deep as she settled into the car a moment later and then adjusted the seatbelt.

"Where do you want to go?" He sat there, staring out at the street in front of him, and waited.

"It doesn't matter, as long as it's quiet."

"Sure." He started the car as he spoke and pulled out. Somewhere quiet, hmm? He drove away from the courthouse and tried to decide where to go.

"Where are we going? Are we heading to your house?" She asked suddenly, panic in her voice.

"It's quiet, I can cook for us, and we can talk without being interrupted."

It was a long moment before she responded, but she finally agreed. "Alright."

"I'm glad I left your insurance alone now." He said, to break the silence.

"Believe me, I am too." She answered, still giving short responses, but at least she was saying something.

"How far along are you?" He asked, getting the one question he wanted to ask the most out of the way.

"A little over five months. I'm as big as a house because there are three of them, although two are bigger than the third one." Keily's hand came up to rub at her stomach and Logan felt…something at the gesture. Something warm that spread out of his chest to the rest of his body.

"Do you know what they are yet?"

"They're babies." She laughed finally, but relented. "Sorry, I couldn't resist. Two are girls, the other one we don't know yet. That one's down here, at the bottom, curled up and always moves when the doctor tries to see what gender it is."

"Ah, stubborn then?"

"A little." Keily relaxed at last and Logan felt some of his own tension easing.

He cut the engine as he pulled up at the house and got out of the car. "What would you like to eat?"

"Whatever is quickest," Keily answered as she struggled to get out of the car. He offered to help but she brushed his hand away. "I can do it."

That's where the baby got its stubbornness from, at least, some of it. He knew he could be just as stubborn, he thought with a smile.

"I can do steaks and salad from a bag."

"Sounds great." She pulled herself up finally and they walked into the house.

He led her into the living room and then decided she knew the place; he'd let her roam as she pleased. "Make yourself at home, I'll just go change and come right back."

"Alright." She agreed and turned towards the kitchen.

By the time he came back, in a pair of black lounge pants and black sweatshirt she already had the steaks on, and wore an apron she'd brought when they were together over her dress. "I was too hungry to wait."

"That's fine, want me to take over?" He offered.

"Yes, please, my feet are killing me." She went over to the table and sat down to take her heels off.

He finished the steaks off, tipped the salad into a bowl, added a few things to make it more appealing, and brought it all to the table. He went back for the salad dressing he knew she preferred, two bottles of water, and put them on the table the housekeeper had set up before he arrived back home for the day.

"Do you need anything else?" Logan lifted an eyebrow and looked over at her with a tiny smile. It was strange to be here with her again, to feel so…calm.

"This is fine, thanks." She said and started to eat.

He watched her while he ate and tried not to think about how much he missed her. How odd it was that he'd started the day dreading seeing her, and now she was here in his house again. He'd wonder how that happened, but her stomach was the answer to that, and an obvious answer at that.

"So, what do you need me to do?" He asked as they finished up their food and sat back from the table.

"What do you mean?" Keily asked as she wiped at her mouth and put her napkin down.

"Do you need money, a place to live? I know you left the apartment…" His voice trailed off as her eyes turned dark and she frowned.

"I don't need any of that, Logan. I'm taking care of myself for once, and the babies. I have a job and a place to live."

"I'm sorry, I didn't mean to imply you didn't." He answered, feeling like an idiot for being so callous. "It's just, they're mine, you said. I'd like to help take care of them, be a part of their lives."

"I'm fine with that, but please don't throw money at

me. That's not why I'm here." She looked him dead in the eye and he could see how tired she was at last. There were hints of dark circles under her eyes and her face wasn't as animated as it usually was.

"I really didn't mean to imply it was, Keily. It took both of us to make them, and I accept that." He pulled his lips in for a moment before he went on. "I'm sorry, I didn't mean to upset you."

"It's fine." She put her hands on her stomach and looked away. "I just wasn't expecting you to take it so well, I guess."

"I'd ask why you didn't tell me, but I know. I guess I should have..." His voice trailed off.

"Should have what, Logan? Asked the woman you'd just left whether she was pregnant? Who would think to do that? Especially a woman you obviously didn't like that much when you ended it." There wasn't an accusation in her voice, just acceptance.

He was stunned she was so calm, but then, it was Keily. She always surprised him. Maybe he should stop underestimating her so much.

"I see your point." He paused and tried to think of what else he should say.

"I don't mind you being in their lives, Logan. To be honest, I'm terrified of what will happen when they're born. The doctor says they'll probably be underweight and there's a risk I'll go into labor early. It's all really quite scary and it would be nice to have you there, when it's time." She paused, staring out of the window on the other side of the table. "I don't mean you have to be, but it would be nice to have you there."

"I'd like to be. And to go to your appointments and everything." He said quickly, leaning over to be closer to her. "I know this is a strange situation, but I'm glad I know now. We can do this together; I know we can."

After thinking about it all day, he wasn't surprised that he was looking forward to being with her for all of this. He was kind of glad he'd found out now, instead of later, after they were born. Should he set up a nursery at the house, he wondered? But then he thought about all the articles he'd seen as he read the news about multiple births being premature and how long they spent in the hospital. He had the money to pay for that, he didn't care about that. What he did care about was making sure they were taken care of.

"Two girls, huh?" He asked, a smile spreading over his face, bringing his features to life.

"Yes, two girls. And one unknown." She smiled a smile that nearly made him gasp, it was so beautiful.

It was a smile of pride, of joy, of love, unlike anything he'd ever seen on her face.

"And you're okay with it? I mean, obviously you are, you're having them, but you've been alone, it couldn't have been easy." He immediately wanted to kick himself for reminding her he'd left her.

"No, actually, I've had Rosa, who I swore to secrecy by the way. You had every right to leave me, so I don't blame you, but I didn't want you to think I'd done this on purpose." Her words stopped and she looked at him, breath held.

"I know you better than that, Keily." He dismissed her worries with a wave of his hand. "I would never think that of you."

"Good. But yeah, I have her, and my sister and I are talking again." She smiled a pleased smile this time and he smiled back.

"That's great news, I know it bothered you a lot that she didn't want to talk to you."

"It did, but we're working on it now. Alice, my niece, is so excited about there being three babies and she can barely stand up herself."

"I bet." He smiled, enjoying watching her talk about her niece. He'd thought Rosa would stick around, but he hadn't known about her sister. He was glad she'd managed to mend that bridge. She really had changed, he decided, although he'd known that all along, really.

"So yeah, I'm not really alone, just not with a man." Her cheeks turned pink and he decided it was best to ignore it. Even if those pink cheeks thawed him a little more.

"You know, Keily, I was a real dick that night I left you." Logan found himself saying.

He'd spent months trying to hold his own emotions back, trying to deny that he really missed Keily and that he hated not being near her. Now that he was with her though, now that he could smell her and see her, he couldn't deny it anymore.

"I would like it if..." He started but she held a hand up.

"Please, don't. If you're about to say what I think you are, please don't. I can't, not right now." She shook her head even though her eyes pleaded with him to make it all better. "I need to concentrate on making these babies right now and, well, I just can't right now."

"I understand." He answered, but it wasn't what he wanted to say. He wanted to ask her to stay, forever.

7

Keily

"My hormones will be the death of me," Keily said to Rosa two weeks later, her feet up on the coffee table at her place.

"Logan's hotness getting to you?" Rosa smirked a knowing grin.

"Why does he have to be so hot?" Keily moaned and faked a sob. "It's killing me."

"I've heard about these pregnancy hormones, how your body just takes over and decides what it wants and how it, um…" Rosa trailed off, her eyes wide as Keily looked at her with narrowed eyes.

"I know. We're all supposed to be crazy and monsters. I think that's partially true lately."

"At least you don't have to go to court anymore." Rosa changed the subject quickly, wisely.

"I know! I'm so glad it's over." Keily sighed. "I can't believe Joe's lawyer had a heart attack."

"I can't either. But the man's a trooper, he got back to work two weeks later."

"Yeah, just in time to see his client go to prison," Keily smirked with glee. "Which is exactly where Joe deserves to be."

"He does." Rosa agreed and leaned over to get her glass of wine from the coffee table. "Sorry I can't share the wine with you."

"It's fine, we're celebrating Joe going to prison. One of us should have a drink, at least."

"You're meeting Logan later?" Rosa broached the subject, her eyes on the cheap wood panel across from the couch.

"Yes, for dinner." Keily moaned and let her head fall against Rosa's. They were sprawled, their heads touching, in the middle of the couch. "I don't want to go but we have to go over some paperwork he wants me to sign."

"What paperwork?" Rosa looked over at Keily, concerned.

"Just a trust fund for the kids or something like that. I told him we should wait for all of that, but he's insisting." Keily rolled her eyes before she went on. "I think he just wants to make sure they're taken care of, but I also think he just wants to see me."

"And that's hard on you because you just want to jump his bones." Rosa grinned, a laugh escaping even though she covered her mouth.

"I so want to jump his bones." Keily agreed and laughed with her friend. "I know I shouldn't, that it's actually the very last thing I should do, but I can't help it. He's just so very good at it and I can't forget that. Especially when he looks at me like he wants to fling me over his shoulder and carry me off to his bed. Or the backseat of his - whatever he wants to fling me over."

"I bet you know exactly what the back of that car is like too." Rosa's grin was wicked this time and Keily lifted an eyebrow at her.

"I do indeed." Keily let her eyes go wide as she remembered that last time in his car. It had been wild, edgy, and a little scary, but she'd been so turned on she could barely stand it. Which only made how much she wanted to get Logan naked now even worse. "I'm going to embarrass myself and do something stupid like attack him in my parking spot. The two old ladies are going to die from shock if they're out walking their dogs this evening."

"You know they will as soon as they see his car. Both of them will suddenly need to take their babies out for one more walk to get an eyeful of Logan."

"I can't blame them. He's good eye candy." Keily smiled with satisfaction, even if she was totally unsatisfied.

She'd told him she wanted to think about the babies right now, to just get through that part, when he'd almost hinted that he wanted her back. She'd done it to save herself some heartache and doubt that would come later. He'd left her once, he might do it again, her brain told her. Her heart wanted to love him while other parts wanted to *love* him. In a slow grinding way that lasted for hours as they…

"Stop that, you're making me feel all hot and bothered now." Rosa interrupted her train of thought and Keily blushed.

"Sorry." She said quickly.

"It's alright. I could just tell what you were thinking, it was written all over your face you dirty girl." Rosa laughed.

"I really can't help it. My hormones are just raging." It was all she could find to blame. Sure, she'd lusted after Logan before, but this was different. This felt like she'd die if she didn't get him to scratch her itch.

"You're not going to last, I can see it now," Rosa said doubtfully.

"I don't know why he'd want me though, I'm as big as a house."

"Some men like that, and besides, couples have sex

all the time while one of them is pregnant. Besides, you're still sexy as hell, girl, don't doubt that." Rosa assured her.

"You have to say that you're my best friend." Keily reminded her.

"I don't have to say it, but I do mean it. If you weren't so caught up in Logan and I didn't have my couple, well, I'd give Logan a run for his money." Rosa was the one with the pink cheeks now.

"Really?" Keily's voice went up loudly, her eyes bright with delight. "I might have let you if I weren't so caught up in Logan."

"We'll never know now," Rosa answered with a shrug. "And that's fine."

"It is. I'm just glad you're my BFF at least." Keily wrapped her arms around Rosa's left arm and snuggled as close as she could with her bump. "I couldn't have got through this without you."

"You're there for me when I need to cry and moan about my couple, or my ex, or my family." Rosa paused to laugh but then went on. "The least I can do is be here for you. And these babies when you have them."

Rosa was the only person allowed to touch Keily's belly and she did so now.

Theirs wasn't a sexual bond, not by any means, it was one of respect and trust, and caring, unlike anything Keily had experienced before. It was only natural she'd let Rosa trace her babies' backs and press against her skin so she could feel their kicks.

"It's so amazing," Rosa whispered, as she always did when she touched Keily's stomach. "I can't believe there's really babies in there, even though I know they are."

"Weird huh?" Keily asked, almost asleep.

"Yeah, but…good too. I was never really sure about having kids and you're having three so I'm not sure I should bother because I know I'll be all over them like they're mine, but, well, it's special isn't it?" Rosa sounded in awe and Keily moved just enough to look at her best friend.

"Yeah, I guess it is. I'm so glad I have you."

"I'm glad to have you. Now go take a nap before that man gets here. You need one." Rosa shooed her friend away. "I'm going to stay right here and make sure you get some rest. And let this wine wear off."

It had only been a bottle big enough to hold two glasses, but Rosa was adamant about not drinking and driving. Keily was the same way and didn't protest as she got up to go back to her bedroom.

An hour later Rosa woke her up and Keily rushed as much as she could to take a shower and get dressed. She deliberately put on maternity pants, harder to access, a white cotton maternity top, and slip-on shoes that were as comfortable as walking on clouds. It wasn't a date, she reminded herself as she left off putting on makeup and tied her hair up in a bun. Not a date.

She was still repeating that mantra as Logan drove them to a restaurant a little while later. He looked good in his wool coat, and she tried to figure out why she always wanted to curl into him when he wore that thing. It was like a beacon to her, drawing her into its warmth, his scent. He wore a black shirt underneath and black slacks that hugged his perfect ass in ways that made her jealous.

Not a date.

She reminded herself again as she tried to concentrate on the menu and order something. She had no idea where they were, didn't care, and didn't care what she ate as long as it came quickly and without much fuss. She couldn't drink wine with dinner, so she settled for apple juice and tried not to look at him.

He needed a haircut but his face was smoothly shaven. His eyes were on his own menu, she saw when she stole a glance at him. There were other people at the restaurant, but she didn't hear them, didn't know they were there, all she had eyes for was Logan.

But this was not a date, and she was not going to sleep with him, and she really needed to stop staring at him like he was the last man on the planet. Even if all she wanted to do was have sex with him at the very first opportunity that presented itself. Even if it was in the bathroom, or on the way home in his car, or once she got home, in her bed. Oh yeah, or bent over the counter in her kitchen, that might work better, he could really…

"Are you okay Keily? You're, um, growling." Logan looked at her, his brown eyes inquisitive and slightly amused.

"Just hungry, sorry." She assured him, and dropped her eyes back to the menu, her cheeks on fire.

"It sounds like it." He chuckled.

Keily glanced up to see what she suspected was a cocksure grin on his face before it quickly disappeared.

Bastard.

He knew what was wrong with her.

He'd been so attuned to her before he left her that she was certain he could smell when she was aroused. He had some kind of intuition and it seemed he hadn't lost that one bit. Damn him.

"And what would you like to…eat, Keily?" Logan asked, voice husky, his eyes boring into hers.

"Asshole." She mumbled but that just made him laugh. It got harder to resist him every time she saw him, and that had been every day since the trial began. He'd been a perfect gentleman, not pushy or suggestive at all. Which made it all the harder for her, because even that respect he gave her decision made him fucking sexy as hell.

"You know, Keily, if there's nothing on the menu that

you'd like I'd always be happy to take you back to my house to...*feed* you." He said as he leaned over towards her across the table, his eyes drawing her in, full of sensual promise. "Or I could do it right here. You know I can."

"Oh." She breathed out, her eyes glued to his. She knew he'd do it too, move his chair right next to her, run his hand up her thigh, to that part of her that ached the most for him. And she almost gave in, until her brain kicked in and made her pull away from his mesmerizing gaze. "I'll have the chicken alfredo."

"I see. Good choice." His voice held a hint of disappointment, but the promise was still there in his eyes.

It was the only choice she could make if she wanted to protect her heart from him. He'd broken it once already; she didn't dare give him another chance at it. Even if that was all she'd dreamed about since he'd left her. How could she trust he wouldn't do it again, just walk without another word?

Well, the babies changed the situation, but still, he had hurt her once and that was enough. It would take more than her hormones to let her heart be broken like that again. She was fairly certain of that. Kind of.

It was really hard to stand her ground when he was so near, even when she was at home and he was at his place. It was really...hard.

Which set off her brain again and she decided to

change the subject. "I have to work tomorrow, my boss insisted since I've missed so many days for the trial."

"They can't penalize you for a court summons," Logan answered immediately, angry at her boss. But he hated where Keily worked now and hated her boss even more. He'd come to the diner, met the man, and immediately disliked him. Keily didn't blame him, she hated the guy too.

"It's fine, Lisa's taken up enough of my slack. She needs a day off." Keily brushed away his worries and smiled. "It's good for me anyway."

"I'm not so certain about that," Logan said but didn't push. It was one area they disagreed on; Keily working at all. He wanted her home and off her feet. She needed to stay busy, even if she was exhausted all the time.

"Well, I am, so we'll agree to disagree," Keily said and put her menu down, at last. She hadn't realized she'd been clutching it like it was a raft in a stormy sea.

"At least we get the satisfaction of knowing Joe will be in prison for a while." Logan broached the one subject they always shied away from: her ex and what he'd done.

"I'm pleased, I have to say. He deserves it after..." Keily trailed off, afraid to say it, of reminding him.

Logan's face didn't turn to anger or stone, it actually relaxed, and he smiled with peace and calm. "He does. Maybe I can get some rest now too."

"What do you mean?" Keily asked quickly, she hadn't known he wasn't resting. He always looked as if he'd slept more than enough.

"Nothing, I just, it's been a long time coming, putting Joe in jail. I'm glad it's over now."

Keily didn't say anything, even though she wanted to ask him so many questions. Did he forgive her role in the mess? What about the other guys there that night? Did he want them to pay too? She would, she did, because she loved him and wanted justice for him. But she was too afraid of seeing that cold hate in his eyes again to ask the questions that she needed answers to.

"What may I get you this evening?" The waiter interrupted them but Keily was kind of glad he did. It meant she didn't have to ponder those awful questions and possibilities anymore.

She told the man what she wanted and waited as Logan did the same. She put on a calm front, but inside she was in turmoil. How was this going to end up? With more heartbreak or peace for them all at last? She had no idea but hoped she'd put a big enough wall up around her heart to protect it. She wasn't sure she could survive it breaking again.

8

Logan

"I'm over six months pregnant, Logan, and I look like I'm about to give birth to a litter of puppies at any moment." Keily moaned as he tried to talk her into going out for dinner. "The last thing I want is to climb in and out of that car of yours. Or mine for that matter."

"I can fix one of the problems you mentioned. Well, both actually. I'll bring dinner to you." He said, a helpless smile on his face. She was very pregnant, after all, and he loved it.

"And the other problem?" She asked over the phone and he could hear the laughter in her voice.

That bothered him, that she was afraid to openly laugh around him. It was something he'd noticed over the weeks since they'd been back in contact with each other. She didn't like to laugh, cry, or anything that might show too much emotion around him. That wasn't to say they didn't laugh together at all, but there was a sparkle to her that was missing now that had little to do with how pregnant she was and a lot to do with how he'd left her. Intuition told him that much.

"Well, I'll need a day or two to rectify the other problem, but I'll see to it." Logan flicked the indicator to turn into a car dealership he was about to pass if he didn't slow down. Keily didn't want to go out because she had a hard time climbing out of either of their cars. He'd get one she could get in and out of without any struggle.

"Hmm, alright. What are you going to pick up for dinner then?"

"I thought Chinese. I'll be an hour or so, I've just got to take care of a few things first. Is Chinese alright?" He asked as he pulled to a stop in front of the dealership. He saw the perfect vehicle right there in the showroom. It was small enough that she wouldn't have to worry about learning to drive a tank, tall enough that she could just step in and out of it, and had enough space for a new mom.

"Yeah, just don't forget the egg rolls."

"I won't." He replied absently, too busy giving a smile to the saleswoman that walked out to meet him as he got out of his car. "I'll see you later, Keily. 'Bye."

"See ya later, Logan." Keily hung up just as the older woman with a name tag declaring her name was Patricia stopped in front of him.

"Hi, I'm Logan Sinclair, I'll take that black Ford Bronco in the display room."

"Oh, very good, sir. Can I show you some of the features?" The 40-something brunette with bright blue eyes smiled congenially at him and led the way into the main office of the dealership.

"Sure, but can you get the paperwork started while we do that?" Logan didn't want to waste time on haggling, he just wanted to buy the car so he could be on his way to Keily.

"This is a relaunch of an older model that's only become available this year." Patricia started but Logan wasn't paying a whole lot of attention.

He'd seen commercials for the car and from visual inspection of the car, he knew it would suit his purposes. What he really wanted was to be back in Keily's presence, not at a dealership listening to the sales pitch.

"You really want this thing, don't you?" The woman asked with an amused smile.

"Yep. Here's my card, put it on that." Logan fished his wallet out of his pocket and handed the card over. "My driver's license, insurance card, and business card."

"Very good. And you don't want to test drive it first?"

The woman looked uncertain but tried to hide it. She didn't want to lose the sale, he could see, but wanted him to be sure.

"Tell you what, put a tag on it, and I'll take it for a spin while you get the paperwork started." Logan watched her eyes light up even more.

"Of course, sir, I'll get these copied and have a colleague put a tag on for you. I'll be right back with the keys."

Logan drove the car to order the food he knew Keily would want. He knew her enough to know sesame chicken was her favorite and she'd never turn it down. He ordered the same thing for himself and put it in the back of the Bronco before he drove back to the dealership. The insurance and paperwork were done by the time he got back and all he needed to do was sign the papers.

"Thanks for this, would it be possible to leave my car here until later on this evening? I'll come back and pick it up later." Logan signed the paperwork presented to him, the sales slip, and stood back up to look at Patricia, perhaps one of the happiest people on the planet at that moment.

"No problem at all. We can deliver the Bronco if you prefer?" She offered, happy to do whatever it took to satisfy Logan.

He smiled a little and shook his head. "No, I've got

the car for my, well, a friend, and I'm headed over there now so if you're good with me leaving my car I'll come back to get it later."

"That's fine. I'll just put the temporary tag on for you and you can be on your way." Patricia nodded and went out to put the tag on. Once she was finished Logan got in and looked around with more interest. It would suit Keily just fine, he decided and drove off to her place.

"You know, you could just go back to the apartment, don't you, Keily?" He asked as he walked into her place a little while later, his eyes roaming over her to check for any signs of distress. She looked the same as she had yesterday, so he set the bag of food down while she shut the door and walked up to him.

"I know, you keep reminding me, but I'm fine here. I kind of like paying my own rent." She pulled out the boxes and then turned to get plates out of a cabinet. She almost knocked over a bottle of cherry lime Sun Drop as she turned but Logan saved it.

"I know, but I'd feel better if you were in a safer area." Logan looked at her with a smile on his face. Apparently, she was so hungry she hadn't noticed he'd pulled up in a new vehicle.

"I'm fine here, Logan, I swear, stop worrying so much." She'd already pulled boxes out of the bag and started to pile food onto plates.

He stood there with the car's remote and key

dangling from his finger. When she turned to hand him a plate with a fork on it, she stopped, her brows furrowed.

"What's that?" She looked up at him before her head went to the window above the kitchen sink, looking out at the car outside. "That's not your car, Logan."

"No, it's not. It's yours. Merry Christmas or happy birthday, as that's tomorrow. Take your pick." He laughed as her jaw dropped and she looked back at him.

"What? Christmas is two days away." She still held the plate out to him, but her eyes were on the car, taking it in. "I can't accept that, shouldn't, but I'm going to because I'm pregnant and hate my car right now."

She took the keys from him, and with the plate still in her hand, walked out to the car.

"Let me take that," Logan said with a pleased smirk, taking the plate from as she opened the door.

"It's so…new!" She breathed and slid into the seat. "Oh, Logan, that was so easy."

"It's got heated seats, which move in all kinds of directions by the way, and all the features this model can have, and that's a lot. I don't know all of them yet because I just bought it and came here."

"And picked up dinner." She made a motion to ask him to give her the plate back and ate carefully while she looked around the car. "I really shouldn't take it…"

"You really should. Those are my babies, their

momma needs a good car that she's comfortable in, and I'll drive it when you can't."

"I guess." She replied then stuck a forkful of rice and sesame chicken into her mouth, making sure not to drop rice on the seat. "It's wonderful, thank you, Logan."

"My pleasure, Keily." He answered and watched her slide out of the car.

"I'll finish eating, then we'll come back out and look it over." She smiled and sighed as she stepped out of the car. "That was so easy to get out of. That's such a relief. I love it, thanks."

"Good, that's all that matters." He answered and followed her into the trailer.

"I'm still not sure I should take it, but I do need something I can get in and out of." She went on, but then took another bite of food as she sat down.

Logan picked up the other plate she'd filled and went to sit on the couch with her. He watched her as they ate together, silent except for the sound of music playing from the television. She wasn't the same woman he'd left all those months ago.

Since then, she'd learned self-reliance and how determined she could be when she wanted something. She was still working, though he didn't want her to. She'd even learned how to say no and mean it, he thought, with a rueful smirk he hid from her.

When they were finished eating, he got up to clean

their plates and forks, threw the empty boxes away, and turned the kitchen light off. He was a man that lived in houses he'd have called mansions as a child, wore tailored suits, bought cars on a whim, and could have anything he wanted. As long as that wasn't Keily, he thought as he looked around the trailer.

What bothered him wasn't that the best she could afford was a trailer, it was that she was alone here. Okay, she had two helpful neighbors, but they were old ladies and he lived too far away if she needed help. And he wanted to help, he wanted to be in her life as more than the man that had fathered her children.

Shame filled him every time he thought about that night that he'd left her, pain tugged at his heart when he remembered how she'd looked at him. Not because the truth had been revealed, at last, but because he'd hurt her. He'd spent months wondering how she was, and now he knew. She was pregnant, that's how she was.

One of his biggest regrets was that he hadn't been there for her when she first found out. She'd been so hurt by him that she'd left the apartment, left him behind. He wanted another chance but didn't want to add to her stress right now. She was…fragile.

It wasn't a term he'd have ever used for Keily when he first hired her to work for him, but since then a lot had changed. They had both changed, but Keily had changed the most, perhaps. Physically, emotionally, mentally, it was a different Keily that he sat beside now.

"Are you going to stare at me all night or are you going to tell me why you're here? Other than the car. You were on your way over here before the car scenario cropped up." She put her feet up on the coffee table and looked over at him, relaxed, happy, calm.

"I just wanted to check on you and the babies." He brushed the question off as if his being there wasn't important. As if he didn't want to beg her to move into his house with him so he could sleep beside her again.

He'd slept better since the trial ended and Joe ended up in prison. He still had the nightmares occasionally, but they were tapering off. He might actually get to do some sleeping beside her, if she'd just move in with him. There was still the worry that sleeping beside her would bring the memories and the nightmares back, but he had a feeling it wouldn't be so bad.

The few hours a day he spent with her now reminded him of why it had been so hard to leave her in the first place. He'd wonder if he loved her, but he wasn't sure he was capable of things like that. His parents might as well have been cold scientists, they'd been so standoffish with him. It was clear from the moment he was old enough to know what it meant, that he was an accident they'd come to regret.

He didn't really know any of his extended family,

and friends had been few and far between over the years. Keily might just be the first person he'd ever felt *anything* for. That wasn't as uncomfortable a thought as it used to be. Months of regret and anger had dulled that discomfort, turned it into a need to have her back with him.

He'd played it cool, acted like leaving her hadn't torn him up inside, but now? He was almost certain that they could build something together, if they tried.

"You're not getting a present as expensive as that car, Logan." She broke into his thoughts and he blinked before he realized what she meant.

"Oh, that's fine, Keily, really. You agreed to come to dinner, that's good enough."

"Hardly." She drawled and looked over at him. "I really shouldn't take it."

"Stop, it's yours and that's all there is to it." He sat up a little straighter and glared at her. That usually worked on people that wanted to argue with him, but it never really did work on Keily, not really.

"You stop that, it'll get you nowhere. It doesn't work on me and you know it." She grinned and leaned over, so he could get a good look at her cheesy grin. "I'll keep the car, but no more, understand?"

"If the babies need stuff or I want them to have something, I'll get it. If it's something you need to help take care of our babies, then I'll get that too. You aren't doing this alone, no matter what."

Even if she wouldn't really touch him now, even if she didn't want to be close to him anymore, he'd find a way to change that. He'd prove to her, one way or another, that he was with her for good now. If that meant he had to be subtle until he won her over, so be it, but he sure hoped she'd give in soon. He missed having her smile at him the way she just had, even if it was only for a moment.

9

———

Keily

"I can't believe this car," Keily mumbled to herself as she synced her phone up with the Bronco's system. She looked at it, not for the first time, impressed with the brand-new vehicle.

There was plenty of space in the back for three car seats, room in the very back for shopping and other things babies needed, and the seats were comfortable. Everything she could ask for, even if she didn't ask for it. She felt kind of bad about Logan shelling out so much money for her, but at the same time, she loved how easy it was to get in and out of. It was much bigger than the company car she'd been driving around in, an economical sedan, but she kind of liked that. She'd driven the Bronco a few times now and every time she felt powerful, being able to see all around and having such a powerful vehicle. She'd caught herself mumbling 'vroom, vroom' a few times now, as she waited at lights.

She was pregnant, she reminded herself, this was one of those times in life that she got to get away with doing things like that. It made her laugh, and she was alone, so it didn't matter anyway. Nobody knew.

The radio played Christmas music throughout the drive to Logan's, but she didn't mind. He was back in her life, although what they were was as precarious and undefined as it ever was. He seemed to want more, but she was hesitant. Did he feel that he owed her something because of the babies? Would he come to resent her later?

There was a night, a night back on that vacation they'd taken in the tropical islands, where he'd let slip that his parents had only been married because his mom got pregnant with him. He'd gone on to tell her how he'd always known they resented him because of it, and that made her even more hesitant. Would he come to regret having children with her?

Not that many people would ever say those words out loud, but would he? In time, he might just walk away from all of them, and she couldn't take that chance with her heart but especially with her babies.

Logan had been patient, gentle, and had even asked to cradle her bump a few times already. He seemed to be enthralled with the fact that she was pregnant, loved looking at her too, even if he did look away when she caught him watching her. He was kind and thoughtful, and that was great, but they never really talked about things that were important. That was partly her fault, and she knew it.

She shied away from promises, from anything that might lead to something more than a hand on her stomach. He looked at her with so much longing sometimes, when he let her see it, and it nearly broke her. She wanted him, she always did, in her bed, in her life, but he'd walked away once already.

When she arrived at his house, Keily parked the car, got the bags out she'd brought with her, and walked into what could only be described as an explosion of Christmas. There were decorations in every room, Christmas trees in every room she walked in, and lights all over the place. It was only midday so she couldn't see the lights outside, but she'd noted the penguins in a globe blow-up decorations, as well as Santa and his reindeer.

Logan came to answer the door and smiled as he let her in. "I've just checked the ham. Dinner won't be long."

"You're cooking?" She asked with a dubious lift of her left eyebrow.

"I am and it's going well. The housekeeper is with her family until after New Year's so I'm doing the cooking and cleaning again." He took the bags from her and walked with her into the living room to put them down. "Want to come in the kitchen with me or do you want to stay in here?"

"I'll follow you," Keily answered and put her coat down on the couch.

The house smelled of baking ham, sweet potatoes, and the sage and rosemary in the stuffing. Dressing, stuffing, whatever, she always called it stuffing, whether it was going into a turkey or not. She saw pies resting on the counter, along with bread rolls, and a few covered dishes. "Are more people coming?"

She looked down at herself and frowned. She was in a blanket with a hole in the top, well, that's what it felt like. It was a dark green dress, a huge fleece dress shaped like an overly long sweatshirt, and black boots she'd struggled to put on. She'd figured out a trick with a wire coat hanger to zip things up, but she wasn't sure even that would work this evening. She hadn't expected to see other people today, not even Rosa or her sister, since Violet was with a doctor she'd met at work and hit it off with. Rosa was with her couple and Keily had been left to fend for herself, so she'd accepted Logan's offer of dinner.

"No, I'm just cooking all of this because it's the kind of dinner I'd order for myself, or have if I went to a holiday dinner. I thought I'd have a go at making it myself. It's been a learning experience."

"Maybe it's best you went for ham instead of turkey in that case. I assumed the housekeeper was going to cook it or something." She frowned at her own assumption and spoke again. "Does she cook?"

"If I'm here she will. She doesn't want me getting too thin. She made the pies before she left, actually." Logan waved at the pies on the counter and Keily smiled as she sat down.

"Something will be edible then." She teased him, and he turned to her with a mock glare.

"It's not all bad, you know. I've had one of the deviled eggs and it was really good. The rest might get thrown away, but those were delicious." Logan's glare eased into a bashful grin. "Actually, I think most of it will be alright. I've been following recipes I found online."

"Hmm, can I have a glass of apple juice please?"

"Of course, but wasn't it giving you indigestion?" He turned to get a glass from the cabinet.

"Not this week, it seems, it's grape juice this week." Keily sighed. "The doctor said I just have to deal with it for now and try to avoid what makes it flare up, but that's hard to do when it changes from day to day."

"You saw him yesterday, didn't you? What else did he say?" Logan had wanted to go but had a video conference with his office in California that he couldn't miss.

"Oh, not much." She hedged, not wanting to tell him exactly what the doctor said. "The babies are fine, growing well for triplets, and I need to, uh, be careful. I may go into labor early since I'm having triplets, and I need to, um, put my feet up at night."

"She told you to stop working, didn't she?" Logan asked with his own lifted eyebrow as he put the juice in front of her.

It was something he'd tried to talk her into since that day at the courthouse. She didn't want to stop working, though. Well, she did, she really did, but he'd also wanted her to move in with him until after the babies came, and that wouldn't work at all. She'd crawl into bed with him, despite how much she felt like a whale, and try to do things she shouldn't. It was hard to control herself when she was at home alone, if she was with him it would be impossible.

"Well." She hedged again, not willing to meet his eyes.

"She did! Keily, you have to stop being so stubborn. Fine, you don't want to live in the apartment, and you don't want to move in with me, but at least stop working."

"I can't have you paying my bills, Logan. I can't." She pouted and glared at him.

She couldn't help it, that was how she felt, like she was being bullied by her doctor and him into quitting work. So, what if her feet, legs, and back would adore it if she didn't go into the diner ever again, but that meant dipping into her savings or taking money from him. Neither of those options were good ones as far as she was concerned.

"Please? It would be the best Christmas present you could give me." He pleaded; his brown eyes full of sadness.

"I'll think about it." She paused to move, two of the babies had decided to kick her, even though she was comfortable for once. That didn't happen often lately.

"Okay. What else is new?"

Keily smiled and told him about Violet's new boyfriend, Alice's new goldfish that her mommy's new boyfriend got for her, and how Rosa was off with her couple. It wasn't something that Rosa was trying to hide, and she'd talked about both in front of Logan a few times he'd been around her with Keily since he came back.

"I'm glad she's happy, Rosa. Well, your sister too, but I've not met her yet so I can't really be glad for her." Logan stirred potatoes on the stove, his back to her.

"Rosa has the best of both worlds, I guess," Keily said absently, remembering their adventures on that island again, that place he'd taken her to. Would she have time for such adventures after the babies came? she wondered. All the mommy groups online went on and on about what hell motherhood was and how you'd never have privacy again but talked about the joys of motherhood at the same time.

Those groups confused and scared Keily, so she'd not been back to any of them for a while now. She knew motherhood wasn't going to be easy, but she couldn't decide if most of those women were silently screaming for help or if they were reveling in each other's misery. It didn't seem healthy, the way they judged each other and the way they talked about their lives, so she'd just started to avoid them.

"It's almost ready, I hope you're hungry, today?" Logan asked and Keily looked up at him with a smile.

"Starving, as usual." She answered and moved again, the pain a throb in her back now. "But I might need a different chair."

"We'll eat in the living room if you want." He said quickly, ready to help her move if she needed it.

"That sounds good. I'm sorry, it's just that my back is hurting."

"Not a problem, let me help you up."

It would be like this, she thought as he helped her up, one hand wrapped around hers, the other out to catch her if she started to fall.

He was always so willing, so ready to help her out and be there for her. She let herself lean into him once she was up and for a moment their eyes met. The gold flecks in his eyes were apparent in the sunlight streaming in through the windows and they fascinated her. They always had.

His eyes fell to her lips and hers went to his. Time stopped and she forgot to breathe. She wanted him to kiss her, wanted to feel him against her, wanted her memories and dreams to be real for once. She leaned into him and almost groaned when her belly got in the way. It was a reminder that she had too much to lose by trusting him to keep her heart in one piece, and that brought her up, away from him.

"Thanks." She mumbled and turned to walk into the living room.

This was a mistake, but she'd known it would be. Between her body wanting to jump his bones and her heart wanting to wallow in his gaze, she was headed for a mistake she couldn't walk away from easily.

"This is why you need to stop working, Keily." Logan sighed as he came in with a plate full of food a little while later. He set up a table for her to eat from and put a glass of juice and her plate on it, along with her fork and knife. "You're in so much pain, and you don't have to be."

She looked at the mound of food on her plate and her stomach growled. Mistake or not, she was starving, and she couldn't turn down what smelled like very good food. Instead of answering him, she took a bite of mashed potatoes and moaned in delight.

What he'd said was true, she was in a lot of pain, so maybe she would give the job up, for now. She hated her boss but liked her coworkers. She'd hate not working with them, but her boss was becoming more than she could deal with. He kept making comments about how big she was, complained that it put her customers off, even though her pregnancy didn't put anyone off at all.

It seemed to make people eager to touch her and talk to her, if anything. They all wanted to feel the baby kick, which she didn't mind, but sometimes it did annoy her, especially when it was a man. Kids and old ladies she didn't mind, grown men she shied away from if they asked. Staying home, putting her feet up, and relaxing for the next three months would be...heaven.

Logan came in and put on *A Christmas Story* to watch as they ate. Ralphie was flopping down the stairs in his pink Easter bunny outfit when the television came on and Keily laughed. It was tradition to watch the film, ever since she was a kid, and she laughed every year, even though she knew what was going to happen.

"I can't wait for our kids to be old enough to watch these old favorites with us." She said after her last bite of food. She wiped her mouth and sat back against the couch. "That was delicious."

"Thank you and yeah, I'm looking forward to watching the kids grow up. It wasn't something I'd really considered, I didn't plan on having a family but, and I know this is hard to believe, I'm really looking forward to having children." He sat back, done with his own plate now.

"Really, Logan? I have worried about it I have to admit." She could already feel sleepiness taking over but had to ask.

"I am, for real. Maybe next week we can pick which room will be their nursery here, actually. We need to get this place ready for them, not just yours." A shadow passed over his face, but he wiped it away.

"Yeah, that might be a good idea." She whispered.

He meant he wanted to have them with him and there'd be times when they'd be at his house. Without her?

That hurt, but what could she say to him? She couldn't deny him his children and if he wanted to spend time with them that was good. So why did it hurt, thinking about him with their babies without her there? And worse, why did it feel right thinking about being here with them all as a proper family?

10

Keily

"I know he means well, but seriously, Violet, he paid my bills. In advance. There are credits on my power bill, water bill, and that's on top of paying for the car and a year of insurance on it." Keily blew air out of her mouth to move her hair out of her eyes and looked over at her sister.

They were at Keily's, sitting on the floor with baby Alice. Keily couldn't make herself stop thinking of Alice that way, even if she was growing up. She'd always be baby Alice. At least until she got old enough to insist her aunt didn't call her that, Keily thought with a sentimental smile. The day would come, she knew that, but hoped it was years away.

"He's just doing what real fathers should, Keily. Don't

complain." Violet said without a hint of malice and softened the words even more by clasping at Keily's bicep with a gentle hand. "Don't get your heart broken but do let him be a dad if that's what he wants. Alice doesn't have anyone as a father figure."

"What about your doctor?" Keily inquired with a gleam in her eyes.

"Maybe, but I've learned my lesson." Violet rolled her eyes and looked over at Alice. "I put my trust in someone before and all I have to show for it is Alice."

"That's not such a bad thing," Keily replied, rubbing at her own belly. She'd learned her lesson too, she hoped.

"I'm just glad he finally talked you into quitting that job, it wasn't good for you, being on your feet all the time like that." Violet's attention turned to Alice as the little girl toddled over to the coffee table to pick up the sippy cup Keily kept on hand for her.

"I didn't want to but even the doctor said it was putting my health and the babies at risk, so I had to give in. I just didn't want Logan taking it upon himself to pay my bills for me. I'm not his woman anymore."

"You might not be my woman anymore, Keily, but I do want what's best for you," Logan said as he came back in from turning the steaks he'd put on the grill outside. She'd decided to have everyone over when the sun came out that morning, warm and full of the promise of spring. It was New Year's Day and what better way to spend it than with the people that mattered the most to her?

Besides, warm days in winter didn't happen often, but every now and then the sun came out and they could have nice times like this. Keily had invited Rosa, but it was Saturday, and she was with the couple that took up so much of her time now.

"Rosa's with her couple," Keily said, to change the subject. Neither Violet nor Logan had asked, but it was a good way to take the focus off of what she hadn't meant for Logan to hear.

"She might be, but that's not the topic at hand." Logan waltzed over to the sink to wash his hands before he came back to the living room and sat down on the couch. "You're not a kept woman, you never were, and you never will be. You are however mine, I mean, *my* children's mother. I will take care of you."

Keily's heart wanted to pound in her chest with pleasure over the way he'd played off that slip of the tongue, revealing his thoughts that she was his, but she told her heart to shut the hell up. She could not afford to let him into that sacred place ever again.

This was going to be difficult, she thought as she absently rubbed at her stomach, lost in her own world, even though he was clearly waiting on an answer. She was his, he'd said. If only that were true.

"You can't fault the man for accepting his responsibilities, Keily," Violet said with a wink in Keily's direction. "Even if that's making sure you have water, power, and a way to get around."

"Stop bullying me, both of you." Keily looked over at Logan and glared at him, her tongue out for a second.

He just winked at her too, and smirked with pleased self-satisfaction.

Bastard, she thought and looked away.

"We aren't bullying you, Keily, we're telling you what's best for you. Even if you don't want to hear it." Violet answered unapologetically. "I've been through this with one baby, I couldn't imagine doing it with three. I don't even know how you're breathing with all those babies in you."

"I know." Keily was glad to let the subject change and leaned back on her palms, her legs out in front of her. "I feel like a beached whale, and they're constantly kicking each other in there."

"Have you thought of names yet?" Violet turned her eyes to her sister for a moment, before she looked back at her daughter, now playing with a child's puzzle on the floor. Alice hadn't quite figured out the object of the game, but she was enjoying banging each large puzzle piece onto the board they fit into.

"Zara, Zoey, and Zinnia, if they're all girls," Keily revealed and was pleased when she saw Logan nod in approval. "I know they're all Z names, and the poor kids will be last in everything that goes in alphabetical order, but I like them."

"What if the bottom baby is a boy?" Logan asked but didn't offer any suggestions.

"Zane?" Keily replied with a questioning look on her face.

"That works," Logan answered with another approving nod.

"I'm glad you like them," Keily said dryly, but with a slight smile.

"I like them too." Violet piped in as she wiped Alice's mouth. She was getting a bit drooly lately, but Violet didn't seem to mind.

"I've got to check the steaks," Logan said suddenly and got up. He left the sisters to carry on talking, the front door open to let the warm air come in.

"You're spending a lot of time together, it seems, but not talking about things you should, I take it?"

"If we did that, Violet." Keily began. "We'd have to talk about things neither of us wants to talk about. Well, things I don't want to talk about."

"Like what?" Violet prodded, her brows together as she looked over at her sister.

"Like why I won't move back into the apartment, and why I don't want to move in with him either. Like what we are to each other, and whether we should be a couple or not."

"I get that," Violet said with a nod of her head. "But, I do wonder if he's not serious this time. The way he talks, I think he might, well, maybe he's in it for real this time."

Violet whispered that last part and leaned over towards her sister, her eyebrow raised in question.

"I think he might be, but after last time, when he left, I just can't go through that again, Violet. It hurt too much and I'm about to have three babies that will take up most of my time. All of my time, really, and where can he fit into all of that? I won't have time for a broken heart or hurt feelings."

"I get you." Violet sighed and tilted her head a little. "I'm thawing towards him, though."

"You would." Keily grinned at her sister and leaned into her to nudge at her. "He's fucking hot."

"Careful." Violet hissed, a smile in her eyes. "Alice is picking up on words now. I'm letting cuss words slip every now and then, and she's picking them up, but I'm trying to stop."

"Oh dear, sorry." Keily sent her sister an apologetic look before she went on. "Anyway, he's hot, nice, respectful, and generous. I'm just not in a place where I can think straight most of the time. My hormones are raging and I don't know whether I'm coming or going. It's not the time to make life-altering decisions."

"I remember that brain fog, it was awful."

"It is. So, I'm leaving decisions until my brain is at least all mine again." Keily struggled to roll over but finally managed to get up to go to the fridge. "Want something to drink?"

"No, I've still got water."

Keily grabbed her own bottle of half-frozen water out of the freezer and sprawled out on the couch.

"Outside, Mommy." Alice insisted and looked up at her mother with hope in her eyes.

"Yes, honey, we can go outside."

"I hope you don't mind if I stay in here, I can't get up again now." Keily closed her eyes and took a drink of the water. It was unseasonably warm, but she wasn't about to complain, not when it was going to be freezing again by the middle of the week.

"Alright, we'll be back in a few minutes then." Keily took Alice's hand and led her out of the door and down the steps.

Keily could hear Alice exclaiming over the things she found in the small patch of grass outside the door. Keily had put some plastic decorations, bumblebees with whirly wings and a few dragonflies with the same, in the now-empty flower bed that ran down the length of the trailer.

It had been a week since that almost kiss at Christmas and things hadn't changed much. Logan had to go to a function a client held for New Year's Eve the night before and Keily had spent the evening alone. It didn't matter if she did want to go, she couldn't stand for long now anyway, without a massive amount of pain in her back and hips. She wouldn't have been comfortable at the party and so it wasn't that much of a big deal when he didn't ask her if she wanted to go.

That was also why she'd finally quit her job three days ago. That and her boss was especially awful the last day she went in. She'd told him to shove his shitty job where the sun don't shine when he made a snide comment about how she walked, and left him without wait staff for the evening. Not that it would matter to him, he'd replace her soon enough, but it was satisfying to tell the idiot off. And to not get up knowing she had to go to work.

All in all, it was nice to know that Logan had and would take care of her. It was nice to relax again, kind of. As much as she could with three tiny humans in her, at least. She wasn't on bedrest yet, though her doctor had threatened her with it if she didn't quit working.

That was another reason she'd quit the job; she didn't want to be confined to a bed for the next couple of months. The doctor said she could get up and move around, but not stand on her feet for too long at a time.

Keily had finally given in and even though she was glad she had that luxury, thanks to Logan, it also twisted her up inside.

Logan was always giving - the car, gifts, paying her bills, but he never asked for anything in return. He always said it was for the good of the babies, but she knew that wasn't all of it. He just used that as an excuse to get her to accept the things he gave.

Keily was glad when her phone beeped, happy for a distraction from the same old thoughts that always led back to…should she give in to her own heart and let Logan back into her life the way he wanted to be?

Sorry I couldn't make it today. Have you managed to get Logan back into your bed yet? Rosa's text asked.

Keily rolled her eyes at the half a dozen emojis Rosa had added to the text. One was an eggplant and even Keily knew what that was - the stand-in emoji for a penis. The text made her laugh anyway.

No, and since you're the one that told me not to let him break my heart again, I'm not sure why you're asking me that. Keily sent back.

I know, but he is hot, and some sex might calm him down at work a little. He's walking around glaring a lot lately. Rosa answered.

Not my circus, not my monkeys, Rosa. You have sex with him. Keily sent the text and immediately regretted it. *No, wait, I take that back. Don't have sex with him. I'd have to hate you both and I love you too much for that.*

Then you're going to have to take one for the team, Keily. Rosa added even more eggplant emojis and a few grins.

Piss off, Rosa. Aren't you busy? Keily added an eye-roll emoji and then a grin before she hit send.

I will be, don't you doubt it a bit.

Keily didn't and, not for the first time, wished she wasn't the size of a house. She'd love to get Logan back into bed, or on the couch, up against a wall, wherever she could. Especially as the sex dreams had ramped up since Christmas. She spent most of her nights tossing and turning because Logan featured in every single dream she had, naked and ready for her.

He walked in the door and she felt her cheeks heat up, even though he couldn't read her thoughts. But maybe that wink he gave her, as if he knew what she was thinking about, meant he did. She glared at him as he turned away, but that only made it worse. Even the smell of the steaks couldn't distract her from how tight his round ass was. Or the mark there that meant she could never be with him.

11

Logan

"Keily?" Logan called out as he walked in her front door a week after their barbecue. She'd called him in tears and begged him to come help her. She hadn't been able to tell him exactly what was wrong, but he didn't ask a lot of questions, he just left his office and sped to her place.

"I'm in here," Keily called out with a shaky voice from the bathroom attached to her bedroom. "Please hand me a towel before you open the shower door."

"What's wrong?" He asked, deflated to find her alright.

"I'm so sorry I called you, but I know Alice has a doctor's appointment Violet can't miss and Rosa is at work. I'm stuck." She said through the stall door, her voice full of tears and embarrassment.

"You're stuck?" He repeated and picked up the huge white towel hanging on the towel rack by the shower stall.

"I'm stuck," Keily answered but drew the word out on a half-wail. "I slipped just after I turned the water off and tried not to fall. I slid down the wall and now I can't get up. This is so fucking embarrassing."

By the time she stopped speaking, she was hiccupping with sobs. She had a bad feeling something like that might happen with how big and clumsy she was right now. Luckily she'd been taking her phone with her everywhere she went, including the shower.

"Oh, Keily, it's alright honey. Here, take the towel." He opened the door enough to hand her the towel. When she took it, he opened the door to see her face red from crying and her eyes full of tears. "It's okay, really, don't cry. Let me help you up."

"I'm fucking huge, Logan. I'll probably hurt your back if you try to help me." She'd draped the towel over her front, but he knew she was naked underneath and he had to admit, she was still as beautiful as she'd always been.

She'd gained a little weight, but it only made her look softer, more appealing. He also had to admit, to himself at least, that it was oddly arousing, knowing she was pregnant with his babies. It was like he'd claimed her body, even if he'd never admit that to her or anyone else, for the duration of the pregnancy. He didn't understand it, so he didn't examine the thought too much, especially when she was stuck in the shower.

"You're seven months pregnant, Keily, stop saying you're huge." He answered instead of examining his caveman thoughts.

"I am huge." She accepted his hand but used one of her own to hold the towel against her body. "Being pregnant caused it and it doesn't change the fact that I'm not a tiny slip of a woman anymore."

"I know, come on, push with me." Logan urged as he leaned over to grab at her back to try to help her off the bottom of the shower. It was hard to figure out how to help her because the truth was, her abdomen did stick out a lot, even if he refused to admit to her that she was huge. The bulge made it awkward to get hold of her, that was all, but he managed it at last and helped her stand up.

"Thanks." She mumbled and swiftly moved away to rearrange the towel. "I'm sorry I dragged you away from the office for this."

"I don't mind a bit. Glad to help." He mumbled. Now that she wasn't crying, the atmosphere in the room turned tense with awkwardness. He rubbed at the back of his head and turned around. She was in front of the door and he couldn't leave the bathroom.

"Oh, um, let me get dressed." She turned and went into the bedroom while he walked out into the living room.

When she came out, dressed in what was basically a long black t-shirt that came down to her ankles, with room for her bump in the middle, he handed her a glass of juice and went to sit on her couch. "Keily, don't you think it's time you came to live with me?"

"I want to say no, again, but after that little incident…" Her voice trailed off, but picked back up once she sat down on the other end of the couch. "I don't want to, but the bigger nursery is there, you'll be around at night, and dammit, I hate it, but yeah, I think it's time."

"I know you like being independent, and I won't intrude on that there, I promise." He knew part of the reason she was so reticent to take help from him was because she'd learned what it was like to take care of herself, properly, for once and she didn't want to give that up.

He knew the main reason was because he'd walked out on her, she didn't have to say the words for him to know that. He'd fucked up and yeah, he might have lived with that knowledge for the rest of his life if she hadn't gotten pregnant. He was man enough to own up to the fact that he probably would have found an excuse to talk to her, to try to repair their relationship, whether she'd been pregnant or not. If only to himself.

He'd had enough time now to wrap his head around the situation, time to take stock of what he really wanted in life, and he wasn't surprised when he came to the conclusion that it was Keily and their children that he wanted. Not Keily *because* of the babies, but Keily *and* the babies.

"You know, Keily, I don't feel like you've trapped me." He stated bluntly, his eyes glued to hers to put weight behind his words. "I know you think I'm a dick, and yeah, I have been, but that's changed now. And not just because of the babies, before that critical brain of yours twists my words up."

He smiled when she blushed and knew that was exactly what she'd been doing.

"I'm not pushing you, you're uncomfortable, you're heavily pregnant, and your tiny frame is overwhelmed. I'm just offering you my help." He stopped talking when tears formed in her eyes. Damn, he'd made her cry. That wasn't what he'd wanted at all. "What did I say?"

"Nothing, it's hormones, that's all." She sniffed and reached for a box of tissues she'd recently put on the coffee table. He had a suspicion her tears were why she had them there. "I've just been humiliated, even if you didn't mind, and now I'm having to accept help again. It's hurting my feelings, that all."

"Well, stop that, you don't have to have hurt feelings at all. Just let me take care of you for now, no strings, no expectations, just a friend helping a friend. Or, rather, a father helping the mother of his children." He twisted his lips and tilted his head a little in a frown of bemusement.

"It is an awkward situation, isn't it?" She finally said after a long pause.

"It is, yes, one we're both responsible for, so would you please stop taking on all the burden and let me help you?" His frown deepened. That was it exactly, he decided before going on. "Those are my babies too, and you're taking away all of the joy of being an expectant father, do you realize that?"

Her eyes went round and her mouth fell open. She blinked a few times and he could see she was thinking it over, perhaps for the first time.

"I guess I have done that, haven't I?" She was the one frowning now and tears filled up her eyes again. "I'm sorry. I just expected you'd think I got pregnant on purpose, or walk away, all the things I've heard about over the years, all the things men have done in the past."

She wasn't making a lot of sense, but at the same time, she was. Women had been put through the wringer throughout time and what else could she expect from someone that had walked out on her before, in such a cruel way? Yeah, he'd been kind of justified, but had he really?

"I know our past is a wall between us, but I've come to realize, Keily, you were a young girl back then. You weren't responsible for any of that. Joe was." He admitted to her, at last. It was the first time he'd really let himself talk about Joe with her.

He knew though, that if he wanted to tear down that wall between them, they had to start talking, before it was too late.

"I'm sorry, Logan." She sniffed again, wiped at her nose, and looked up at him, exhausted, miserable, and full of sadness. "I can't ever forgive myself for leaving you that night."

"Hush, woman." He looked away, overcome by her apology. "There wasn't anything you could have done. We were both outnumbered and it was just, well, it's the past."

He wanted to push the memories back into the past, wanted to do away with them altogether, to bring the moment back to now, despite his thoughts only moments ago. It was still a painful subject, sore and infected with fear he didn't want to relive. "Anyway, let's pack up some of your clothes and whatever else you need. Are you back in class this week?"

"No, I decided not to chance it and I've taken a leave

of absence for a semester. Since I don't need financial aid or anything, I can get away with two semesters, if I have to. I didn't want to, but, babies." She said simply, pointing at her distended belly with a hopeful but still sad smile.

"You'll get back to it." And he had no doubt she would.

An hour later they had his car and her Bronco loaded up with what she absolutely had to have, and he'd talked to the landlady. Logan didn't tell Keily, but he paid for six months of rent to keep the place open for her, in case she wanted to come back. And he had to admit as he followed her back to his house, she'd seemed more comfortable at that trailer than she had anywhere else he'd been with her.

That was likely because she paid for her bills, but he also thought the humble surroundings made her proud of what she'd accomplished. Yeah, she was in a trailer, but it was the place she'd made her home. The only reason she was even agreeing to move in with him was because she needed the help. The small guest room was too small for him and the trailer was too small for them to live in without getting in each other's way.

There was plenty of room to spread out at his house and for them to maintain the distance she was desperate to keep between them. If she weren't pregnant, he'd just sweep her up and kiss her protests away. He'd whisper whatever it took, as long as it was true, to get her to be his again.

For now, he'd wait, not stress her out, and let her have some peace. The housekeeper would be there to help her during the day and in the evenings, he'd be there to keep an eye on her. She wouldn't be alone and could relax, knowing someone was always there to help.

And maybe he'd get to take her defenses down, one by one, without her noticing.

Logan smiled as they pulled into his driveway and he helped her into the house. She looked back at him as he took her to a bedroom just across from his. He knew she remembered being in his room, the things they'd done in there. The things they could do again, if she'd only give him one chance to prove he could be what she needed.

For a moment, he thought she was about to speak, but then she turned away. Logan felt his heart lurch in his chest when she opened the door without a word and walked into the bedroom. The moment was gone before it had even started.

He brought up everything she'd packed but had to get back to the office before he could unpack for her. "Judith will come and help you; I'll see you later, Keily. Buzz me if you need anything before I come home."

She smiled a thank you as he turned away and left her.

It was late before he got home that night, and she was asleep. He ate the dinner left in the fridge for him and went to bed, too tired to do anything more than check on Keily. She was asleep, peaceful from the looks of it, so he slipped into his inviting bed and fell asleep.

The dream came in the darkest hours of the night, the flicker of flames at the edges of his vision a trigger for his heart to start pounding. No, not again, he thought vaguely, but the nightmare carried on, always the same, until he screamed himself awake. Only, he wasn't alone when he woke up.

"Keily?" He asked, despite his pounding heart and rapid breathing.

She'd wrapped her arms around his head, and he was cradled as well as he could be against her body. His head was still spinning from the dream, still a whirl of emotions and fear, but he clung to her, unwilling to let go of the anchor she'd become the instant he woke up.

"It's okay, Logan. It was just a bad dream." She whispered to him, her right hand stroking his head gently as she kissed him right by his left ear. "It's okay, go back to sleep."

Logan stared at her as the fear passed, as the sweat on his body cooled and dried up, seeing only her outline in the darkness. She felt like home, like his woman, like the comfort he'd needed all this time. He should have recognized that before, back before he'd fucked their lives up and walked out on her. But he was too tired to cling to the moment, to his thoughts, and it felt too good, being in her arms.

Logan turned his head to kiss her jaw, wrapped an arm around her nightgown-clad body, a white thing that she loved but wasn't meant for seduction. If he hadn't been so exhausted, he'd have told her it might not be meant for seduction, but it was seductive because she had it on, but he was tired, needed sleep.

With their bodies almost entwined Logan fell asleep and found peaceful rest at last. He dreamed about babies, about taking Keily to heaven and real places on Earth, he dreamed of being happy, and slept without fear for the rest of the night. He'd had the nightmare beside her in bed before, but when he woke up the next morning, he knew that the memory that haunted his dreams would haunt him no more. Keily had conquered it with the love she was afraid to give. He had to find a way to show her now that she could count on him, that she'd have just as much love and happiness in return, if she'd only give him a chance. Maybe after the babies came, she'd find her way back to him. Or maybe he'd find the words, at last, to show her that was all he ever wanted or needed.

12

Keily

Keily felt a cramp deep in her abdomen, something that twisted and pulled at her insides with brutal carelessness. The doctor warned her about Braxton Hicks contractions and how she might feel the false labor pains, especially now that she was in the eighth month of her pregnancy.

She'd already sent a message to the doctor's office, and she knew she'd get a call soon, if she didn't send another message. Logan was at work, but she was about to call him when the contraction started, long, powerful, painful enough to make her groan loudly. Thankfully, Judith heard her in the living room and came rushing in.

"It's not Braxton Hicks, is it, Keily?" Judith asked, the

housekeeper now on familiar terms with the woman that had moved in with her boss.

"I don't think so, Judith. Can you call an ambulance for me? I think it would be best to have them take me to the hospital. And text Logan, please." Keily whooshed the words out between the panting breaths she took, trying to ride out the never-ending wave of pain. "Fuccccck."

It was a growl of pain, a plea for the pain to end, but it didn't. It carried on until she thought she'd pass out. By the time the pain did stop, Keily was out of breath, wondering why she was wet.

"Your water's broken, Keily. The ambulance is on the way. What can I get you?"

Keily looked around to see her left hand clasped in the housekeeper's, who was kneeling in front of her. "You're so sweet, Judith. For now, I guess nothing. Except a dry dress, but they'll soon take that off me when I get to the hospital."

"They will, but I'll fetch you one if you want a dry one, Keily." Judith let go of her hand and raced up the stairs before Keily could protest.

By the time the ambulance arrived, Keily was screaming, in a dry gown, but screaming. Judith was in tears, not from Keily crushing her hand, but from watching the young woman go through so much pain. Keily knew this was going to be painful, she'd heard her whole life that birth was a pain unlike any other, but she'd had no clue just how soul-consuming that pain was. It took every thought in her head away, centered her in a dark place where all she could do was cling to breaths and hope the pain would pass before it consumed her.

Another flash happened, a blink of her eyes and she saw Logan pull up with Rosa in his car, just as the paramedics loaded Keily into the ambulance and she reached for him. He flew out of the car, asked which hospital she was going to, and pulled out so the ambulance could back up and get on the road.

Everything became a blur after one of the paramedics put an IV in her arm. She heard words as she was unloaded from the ambulance, tried to follow instructions as Logan took her hand, his eyes huge and full of fear. He was the anchor she needed in this rushing storm of pain and confusion, and he was there, despite the red fear that flushed his cheeks, despite the tears that streamed down his face as they wheeled her into a bright white room full of sounds that only confused her more.

"I'm here, Keily. I'm here, baby. It's okay." He kept repeating for what felt like hours. "I'm here, baby. I'm here."

The pain faded, the world faded, as somebody placed a mask over her face. Keily heard words that sounded like emergency C-section, but she wasn't sure. Everything had fallen to pieces the moment she woke up in pain that morning. Her birth plan, the calls she'd planned to make to her sister and Rosa, had all gone out the window, but she'd known to expect that. This was her first pregnancy, and it was multiples, she knew better than to plan anyway.

Darkness held her in its grip, a darkness she couldn't escape from. Her sister's voice intruded into that darkness, pulled her back to the world, but the darkness rushed up to grab her back. Logan's voice this time, and Rosa's, all of them begging her to come back, to wake up, but the darkness would not let her go.

It was terrifying, how much she just wanted to give up and let that darkness take her. Even when she heard a baby's cry, when she knew that voice was her child's, she couldn't break the hold that darkness had on her. Until she heard Logan's voice, one last time.

"You can't leave me, Keily. You just can't." There were tears in his voice, and she didn't know if it was real, or another trick of the darkness, but she felt her soul move towards his voice anyway, trusting that it was him, that he was calling her back to the world. "I love you, Keily, please, come back to me."

Her eyes popped open so suddenly it left her surprised. She was in a dark room now, Logan's hand still in hers, his head beside her on the bed. The noise was gone and everything was…too quiet. Her blurry eyes connected with the clock on the wall and she saw it was sometime after 12. Midnight? It must be, since it was dark outside the window of her room. "Logan?"

Her voice was a soft croak that did nothing to make him move. Even the fragile touch of her hand against his hair didn't make him move. She looked around and saw Rosa and her sister were asleep on a couch at the other end of the private room Logan had paid for before she'd even arrived at the hospital. For a moment, she felt that her body wasn't her own, she didn't recognize the sensations her nerves messaged to her brain, but then it dawned on her. It was the drugs. She was in the hospital.

Her hand went to her stomach. It wasn't flat, not yet, but she didn't feel her babies in her. "Logan?"

His name came out stronger, with more force and this time his head lifted from where he'd fallen asleep. "Keily?"

His face was exhausted, unshaven, confused, but his eyes so warm and crystal clear.

"What happened? Where are the babies?" She was almost afraid to ask the question, a fear she'd refused to allow at the forefront of her mind. She would not think it, but she'd fear it in a primal part of her soul that knew better, that knew she didn't deserve to be happy.

"Two are in the nursery. The smallest is in the NICU until she's out of the woods. Her lungs aren't developed enough yet. Her pediatrician is pretty confident she'll be okay, though. How do you feel?" He stood up to brush sticky hair away from her face, to kiss her forehead, before he pulled away.

"I'm okay. I guess it's the drugs. Just thirsty."

"Here's some water," Violet mumbled as she and Rosa got up from the couch and came over to Keily. "I'll go get some and let the nurse know you're awake. Welcome back to the world, Mommy."

Keily saw her sister's proud smile and felt pride rush into her as a flush of warmth that brought tears to her eyes. "Thanks."

Rosa came over, pecked her cheek, and rushed out of the room, hiding a sob as she left.

"What happened?" Keily asked, confused by what had just happened with Rosa.

"You scared the fuck out of us Keily. There were..." Logan paused and looked down at where his hand was still wrapped in Keily's. "There were complications, and you lost a lot of blood. The doctor couldn't control it and I'm afraid he was forced to perform a hysterectomy. You won't be able to have more children, Keily."

"Oh." She answered, confused about why that didn't seem so important now. "But I'm not dead?"

"No." Logan laughed softly. "You aren't dead."

"That's why it doesn't seem important then." She

smiled, relieved to be alive and awake. "Being dead is worse than not being able to have more children."

"I know, that's what I thought." Logan stood up to sit beside Keily, his eyes examining her. "I guess the doctor can explain it better, but your uterus was damaged by the placenta of one of the girls, and the bleeding wouldn't stop, so they had to do it, Keily."

"I might be upset about it later, Logan, but right now, the girls are in good hands and so am I. I can't be upset right now, I really can't." She looked around, hoping the babies would soon be in sight.

"Maybe it's the drugs you're on too." Logan pointed up at the stand that held several bags of drugs, all dripping into an IV in her arm.

"Maybe. I want to see the girls." She looked up at him, a plea in her eyes.

"I'll get the nurse to bring them in." Logan started but a nurse soon bustled in and pushed him out of the way.

"You can see your gorgeous girls once I check you over, madam." The nurse, her name Joan according to her nametag, pulled blankets away to check stitches, looked for signs of blood or infection, and recorded Keily's vitals before she stood back with a pleased nod. "Alright then, I'll bring the girls in to you."

"Except the smallest one, Logan said?" Keily said and the nurse nodded.

"Baby C, as we're calling her for now, has been put

into NICU. You may be able to see her in the morning. She's doing well though, I checked before I came in because I knew you'd want to know."

"Thanks," Keily mumbled, concern creasing her forehead. The smallest baby, the one she'd worried about throughout the pregnancy, was fighting her way to life. Keily wanted to see her badly, a need unlike anything she'd ever felt before, but she controlled herself. For now.

Two other nurses brought in the two bigger girls, both still small at five pounds nine ounces and five pounds three ounces. "They're so tiny."

Keily was almost afraid to breathe around them. Not only were they early, they were tiny, but breathing and thriving on their own so they had been taken to the nursery. Keily followed the instructions the nurse gave her and took one baby while Logan took the other. "Let me see yours, Logan."

Logan sat down with the little baby girl in his arms and held her out so that Keily could see her. "They're so pretty."

"And identical," Logan added. "They all are."

"That's even more rare." Keily laughed a little. "Maybe it's best I had the hysterectomy. If I lucked out the first time, I'd hate to see what happened if I got pregnant again. I couldn't do multiples again, no way." It was a coping mechanism, perhaps, to laugh at a time like this, but she didn't know what else to do. While she felt complete joy at seeing two of her girls, one was in intensive care and that broke Keily's heart.

"You survived, that's all that matters," Logan responded and held the baby closer to his heart.

He was distracted with the girl so Keily looked at the baby she held. A tiny little scrunched-up face with blonde hair hidden under a knit cap, and tiny little limbs made up the little girl she loved instantly. She loved them all, but this was the first one she'd held. Now she had to figure out their names.

"Shall we do them in alphabetical order?" Logan asked, again reading her mind.

"Maybe. Does she look like a Zara?" Keily moved the baby so that Logan could see her more clearly.

"Definitely." He nodded and started to soothe the baby that began to fuss in his arms. "And this little flower is Zinnia, then?"

"I think so." Keily nodded. "And our baby in the NICU is Zoe then?"

"Sounds delightful to me, Keily. Our first joint decision as parents. Well done us." The baby started to fuss even louder, and he looked to her for help.

"I don't know. Hungry maybe?"

The nurse waltzed back into the room and looked at Keily. "I'm not going to give you any grief after what you've been through, but you have to decide. Breastfeed or formula? I'd suggest, if you don't mind, that we at least pump milk for the baby in NICU."

"Zoe," Keily replied instantly. "She's Zoe, my daughter that's in the NICU."

The words 'my daughter' felt strange but good. She liked saying them.

"I'll put their names on their charts if you've decided?" Joan said, her dark eyebrows arched over her eyes quizzically.

"I have, and if I can breastfeed these two and Zoe, I'd like to," Keily said with an uncertain look.

"You can try but we need to keep an eye on them. Let me help you." Joan brought over a pillow that Violet had bought for Keily and put it in her lap. "Put her head here."

"This one is Zara," Keily said. "That one is Zinnia."

"Very nice, okay, let's put her here, Dad, shall we?" Joan directed Logan as to where Zinnia needed to go and helped Keily until both babies latched on and began to feed with hungry little snorts.

"Are you alright?" Joan asked, waiting for Keily's questions or concerns.

"It just feels strange, but it's also a relief. I didn't realize how sore they were."

"Is this safe with the medicine she's been on?" Logan's concern wouldn't let him remain quiet.

"Yes, most of the drugs have left her system, and

those still running through are alright." Joan paused to reposition Zoe's head a little and then stepped back. "Now, don't be disappointed if it's hard at first, or you don't have a huge supply. You have had a major surgery, had to have a blood transfusion, and you've been through a lot. Give yourself time and be patient. And don't be afraid to ask questions."

"Thanks." Keily glanced up at Joan, but couldn't take her eyes off the babies. Her heart grieved for the baby that wasn't there, but she managed her emotions, by some Herculean effort.

"I'm so proud of you, Keily," Logan said and sat down to watch her with their babies. "You've just, I don't know, you made my world turn upside down and then you set it right again."

It was at that moment that she remembered how many times he'd whispered that he loved her. But was that the drugs or had he really said those things? For now, all she could do was take care of her babies and see what happened later. And maybe hope that this would all work out, somehow.

13

———

Logan

Having children changes the world for you, Logan thought eight weeks after the world turned completely upside down. He'd spent so many days in the hospital with Keily and Zoe, their smallest little girl that he'd come to think of the hospital as his second home. Things were looking up though, and there would be no more daily trips to the hospital because they were bringing Zoe home, at last.

"I'm so happy." Keily sighed with a smile full of bliss on her face. She'd had that look often since she came home from the hospital, but this time it wasn't marred by the shadow of worry she'd carried around with her since the day the girls were born.

"I am, too. It'll be nice to be home with all of our

girls." Logan glanced over to catch Keily's reaction, but she'd turned her head away to look out of her window of the Bronco. Zinnia and Zara were in the backseat in their car seats, dreaming baby dreams.

All the girls put on weight at a surprising rate, and Zoe had improved quickly over the days. Keily had problems feeding all of the girls at first, but once she'd started the girls on formula to supplement their intake that seemed to work wonders for them all. Zoe had gone from the NICU to a regular room and now they were going to bring her home, at last. Their little family was complete.

Even if, at the back of his mind, he wondered when Keily would tear their family apart and move back to the trailer. She hadn't mentioned it, seemed content to play house at his house, and he wasn't about to bring the topic up. If she was happy at his place, then he wouldn't rock the boat.

They arrived at the hospital and went up to the pediatrics floor. Zoe no longer had tubes and wires connected all over her body and she was looking around, kicking her tiny little feet in the onesie she had on. Her blonde hair and gray eyes matched her sisters' and her mother's. They were the spitting image of Keily, and he adored them more for that, perhaps, than if they'd looked even a little bit like him. He adored their mother, so it was only logical he'd adore her three little clones.

Logan picked Zoe up when the nurse said everything was done and asked Keily to sign some papers. He stared down at her, his heart expanding in his chest until he thought it would burst with love. Love was a word he'd long been uncomfortable with but now that his girls were in his life, well, that had changed. He told all three of his babies that he loved them, every chance he got. Which was often since he had started working from home most days.

He'd go into the office if he needed to, and he put things Wally couldn't handle on hold in California so that he could help out at home. Judith was around a lot, as were Rosa and Violet, but he wanted to be there with his children, so they'd know from day one that they were loved, wanted, and special to him. He didn't want them to grow up as he'd done, knowing he was nothing but a mistake and a burden.

"She's so much heavier now," Logan said to the nurse as he brought Zoe up to his heart and laid her against his chest. Her tiny little head nuzzled at him for a moment before she sighed with contentment. He and Keily both had spent hours with her, skin to skin, learning what it was like to care for a preemie that was only four pounds when she was born.

He'd never felt so big and ungainly as he had the

moment he'd held Zoe for the first time. Her sisters were small too, but Zoe had been the smallest, the most fragile of them all and he'd learned quickly how to be as gentle as he could possibly be. It was all overwhelming at first, but he'd learned, and he was an expert now at not only telling them apart but picking up even the smallest change in each girl.

"She is, and a happy girl too." The nurse replied before she took the papers from Keily. "I guess that's all. We've all said our goodbyes to Zoe, all of us that have taken care of her over the last few weeks, and we all wish you the best. It's been a pleasure."

"Thanks." Keily and Logan said together, only Keily had tears in her eyes.

"Shall we go home?" Logan asked and Keily nodded. Logan put Zoe in her car seat and picked up Zara in her own seat. Keily latched an arm under Zinnia's seat and they finally left the hospital together, all of them.

"I can't believe it's finally over with," Keily said as she buckled Zinnia's seat in and got in her own seat. "I thought this day would never come."

"It was hard, but you've done well and so have the girls. We can relax a little now, I hope." Logan laughed before he went on. "Not that there's any time to relax but we can breathe easier, I think, knowing they're all well enough to be home."

"I know what you mean," Keily reassured him. "It's going to be controlled chaos, I think."

"We're used to that," Logan said and for some reason that night she'd soothed him back to sleep after the nightmare woke him up came back to him. He hadn't had that awful dream since that night and he wondered if Keily had healed him. She'd given him a new purpose in life, brought him the three most wonderful gifts he'd ever been able to call his own, and the nightmare was over.

Now, he just had to convince her to stay.

"You've got it under control," Logan added and meant it. She was efficient but so loving with the babies. He'd never seen so much love on her face as he had when she was with the girls. Keily was a good mother and he was glad for that.

"You and Avery help a lot with that, you know?" She countered, her smoky gray eyes on him, full of pride. "You are surprisingly helpful."

"Because I'm a man? That's sexist, Keily." He sniffed imperiously as he pulled into the driveway but spoiled it all with a laugh. "No, you're right, I'm more hands-on than I thought I'd be. I've always heard women say how they fell in love the minute they saw their babies, but I didn't know it happened to men too."

"I guess it doesn't always happen that way, for men or women. Our girls are lucky you're their dad." She climbed out once he'd turned the car off, and had her handbag, the diaper bag, and another bag slung over one shoulder while she wrestled with the seatbelt to get Zinnia out.

Zinnia was the most cheerful of all the girls, while Zara was quiet, serious, often looking at him with such serious scrutiny that it made him laugh. She seemed to be judging him and finding fault with him most of the time, poor girl. But she would cuddle up with him when he tried to soothe her, the few times she'd fuss, and always smiled at some point, as if to take away the sting of her judgment.

Zoe was a mixture of the other two girls, cheerful and full of smiles most of the time, she would sometimes slip into Zara mode when she was tired or cranky. Still smaller than her sisters, Zoe would probably always worry them the most, but she was catching up, so maybe there wouldn't always be this dread in the back of his mind that something was about to go wrong. Or maybe not, he decided as he managed to get Zara and Zoe out of the car and up to the nursery. He was a father now, a real one, and he somehow doubted that dread would ever leave him.

"We're all home, Avery," Logan called out and the nanny he'd hired burst out of her room with a face wreathed in smiles.

"Oh, I'm so excited to meet Zoe." She said with an Irish lilt in her voice.

Avery was the newest edition to his staff; one he'd hired the minute he figured out they needed help with all three girls. He'd called a staffing agency and looked through files until he found the right woman to help them. In her 50s, Avery was a tall, plump woman with soft hands and laughing eyes that could be firm when they needed to be and soft when that was called for. He'd interviewed her the day after the girls were born and found her to be perfect for the job.

Keily had protested having a nanny at first but soon came to agree, they needed help. Neither one of them knew anything about taking care of babies and Avery came armed with knowledge that Keily had kept asking Violet for. She'd eventually seen that calling Violet every five minutes was going to make her a nuisance, so she'd given in to the idea.

Avery headed straight for Zoe and took her out of the car seat with wide, gentle hands. "Oh, aren't you a pretty little thing?"

Logan smiled as Avery cooed over the little girl and took Zara out of her seat. Zara laughed with delight and kicked her feet as her daddy put her up against his chest. "And how are you, my little angel?"

She laughed as an answer before he realized all her kicking and giggling had led to a dirty diaper. He was an experienced diaper changer now and had her changed and buttoned back up in no time. He looked around to see Keily was feeding Zinnia which meant it would soon be Zara and Zoe's turn.

Zoe, unlike her sisters, had never managed to latch on properly so she was bottle-fed milk that Keily pumped for her. Feeding the girls was something Keily had been passionate about, and that hadn't changed. They were getting more and more formula as time went on, but Keily was logical enough to admit that she couldn't keep up with feeding all three of them.

Zoe started to fuss, and Avery moved to prepare a bottle for her. The nursery was set up to handle anything the girls might need, except for a washer and dryer. There was even a small kitchen to one end of the large room filled with three rocking chairs, three changing tables, three cribs, and three of everything else Logan thought the girls might want or need.

It was only later that day, after the girls were in bed for the night and Keily had changed into a set of pink pajamas, that he finally looked at Keily with anything more than concern over how she was feeling. She'd lost a large portion of the baby weight she'd picked up, her eyes were no longer outlined in dark smudges, and she looked happy. She had no makeup on, her hair was in a messy bun, and her socks didn't match, but she'd never looked more beautiful.

To him, she was a goddess, a woman who'd given life to three of the most beautiful girls on the planet and was more than capable of taking care of them. He'd only supplied the help because he didn't want her to struggle and they both needed the knowledge Avery came armed with.

"How are you feeling?" He asked and sat down on the small couch in her bedroom. Their relationship had relaxed enough after she came home from the hospital that he'd walk into her room, as long as her door was open, without knocking. If the door was closed, he'd knock or leave her alone. She did the same with him.

"I'm tired, but happy, Logan." She sighed and leaned back against her headboard; the book she'd been reading forgotten. "It's so nice, knowing they're all home now."

"It's wonderful, really." He agreed and sat back, ready for a long talk, if she was willing.

"What's up, Logan?" She looked at him quizzically, her eyebrows arched together. "Is everything okay?"

"It is, I've just got a lot on my mind." He waved off her concern, not ready to ask her to stay, to be his wife, to spend the rest of her life with him and only him. Well, he was ready, but she wasn't, and he knew it.

"Such as?" She leaned forward to put her arms around her knees as she sat up, her head tilted to the left.

"Just, what the future holds for all of us." He

shrugged, knowing he should broach the subject more carefully, but the words had slipped from his tongue without him even thinking about them. "Where will we be next month, a year from now, ten years from now?"

"I don't know, Logan." She paused, looked down at her knees, covered in pink flannel, and frowned. "Everything's upside down at the moment, isn't it?"

"It is. And you haven't really had time to recover from it all. Oh, I know it's been eight weeks, but your body is still healing, as is your mind." He paused, wondering if he'd overstepped his bounds. She didn't protest, just looked at him with curiosity, so he went on. "Everything has changed for you. You're a mother, but you can't have any more children now and well, that has to be hard for you."

"I guess it's not an issue right now. I have three girls to take care of, more than I ever thought I'd have, you know? I wasn't planning to have babies, not until it happened." She paused this time, frowned deeper, but then looked up at him with clear eyes. "Maybe one day I'll be sad over what happened, but my girls came out of it all. I can't regret that."

"I'm glad you feel that way." He came to a stop, not sure what to say next. "If you want to talk about it, I'm here, you know?"

"I know, Logan, and thank you, but really, it's not an issue at all right now. Like I said, maybe one day I'll have time to sit down and regret not being able to have more children but right now, it's more of a relief than anything. I can't imagine going through all of that again, honestly."

"Okay. Well, I guess you want to get back to your reading." He got up and went to the door. "Good night, Keily."

"Good night, Logan. Thanks for checking on me." She smiled at him and for a second, he saw longing on her face, as if she didn't want him to go. The look faded though, and he left her to her peace and quiet.

Another week or two, that's what he'd give her, then he'd show her how much he wanted things to change for them. He'd show her he could be the man he should have been all along.

14

Keily

Keily woke up the next morning feeling as if she'd slept for a change. Avery, Logan, Rosa, and Violet were always around at different times to help out, but she'd worried about Zoe so much she'd been restless most nights. She'd watch over the two girls that were home with her on the worst nights, nights when Zoe was showing signs of distress or hadn't had a good day, but she was healthy now and home.

And she could get out of bed without pain now, which was a minor miracle in itself. Keily threw her covers off and went to the bathroom to shower. Once she'd managed that and put on a slouchy dress, she went in to check on the girls. It was a habit she'd forced herself into when she got home from the hospital. The lactation consultant reinforced cleanliness, even when her first instincts were to pick up whichever baby was crying and feed them.

She settled into a chair once she'd checked on each girl and saw they were still asleep. As the sun began to rise in the sky, she pumped milk for Zoe and then went to pick up Zinnia. The happy baby waved her arms as her mommy picked her up. Keily couldn't help but smile back at her daughter as she settled down with her in a rocking chair. Zinnia was still hungry by the time Keily heard Zara wake up.

Avery was there by then, ready to help, and picked up Zara to soothe her while she prepared a bottle for the baby. Logan came in and pulled Zoe up to bathe her and put fresh clothes and a diaper on her. He then sat down to feed her one of the bottles Avery handed to him. Keily watched him, as she'd done so many times since the babies were born.

Her hormones were still fluctuating but when he walked in a room they seemed to go into a rage, ready to tackle him and pull his clothes off. Every time he kissed one of their babies or picked them up or simply smiled at them, her body went into some kind of meltdown that melted into love mixed with desire. She'd thought she loved him before the babies came. Now? She couldn't imagine loving him more than she did now.

What she'd felt before was nothing compared to how

she felt about him now. He turned, catching her gaze as she stood up with Zinnia in her arms. His face was a mask of awe as he looked at her and she wondered, not for the first time, if Logan had changed as much as she had.

Two years ago, she wouldn't have thought it possible to be caring for three babies at once, while dealing with the aftermath of a hysterectomy. Her uterus had suffered catastrophic bleeding that would have only been worse once the placenta was removed. She'd read since that day that the problem should have been picked up by ultrasound, but it hadn't been. She was a little angry about that, but what she'd said to Logan was true, she had too much to worry about, too much to do, to think about the fact that she'd lost the ability to have more children.

Besides, her girls were enough. She'd never felt so maternal, didn't think she could, until the day she had them. When the first baby was placed in her arms hormones flooded through her, taking away any twinges of pain, taking away thoughts of future pregnancies. She didn't want to have more children anyway, if they weren't Logan's.

He'd been a rock throughout the whole ordeal, even though he'd never repeated those three little words she wasn't even sure he'd actually said. Every now and then, she'd catch him looking at her as he'd just done, with something like awe and adoration on his face.

He kept saying he was proud of her, but she was prouder of him. He'd been there every step of the way, even staying with Zoe at the hospital when Keily was nearly on the verge of collapse. She'd tried to spread herself out, to spend as much time with the baby in the hospital and the babies at home and he'd finally insisted she stop overextending herself and let him help.

"They're my children too, Keily, Zoe's mine as much as she is yours. I want to be there with her, for her. Let me do this. I can do it, you know?" He'd brushed hair out of her face as she'd wept with exhaustion, wanting to sleep but not wanting to leave Zoe.

Until then she'd stayed, whether Logan was there or not, but after that, she let him take some of the load off of her shoulders. She'd relaxed a little and now, they were all home, safe and sound.

Maybe it was time to move on to other subjects, address other matters in their lives?

She smiled down at Zinnia as the baby splashed in her tiny infant tub and blew spit bubbles at her mommy. "You're such a bad girl, Zinnia, just like your mommy."

Keily stroked a hand down her daughter's face, admiration and love alive in her eyes. Zinnia was her troublemaker, she could tell that already, the one that would talk the other two into doing naughty things they shouldn't. The most like her, really, Keily thought with a silent laugh.

Rosa and Violet showed up a few hours later and Keily watched little Alice check each girl before she settled down to watch television on the couch in the nursery.

"How's everything going?" Rosa asked as Logan left to get some work done in his home office.

"Fine, really. Zoe's doing well and the other two are as well." Keily had all three babies on a quilt on the floor, playing with them all as they wobbled back and forth looking at each other. They couldn't roll over very much yet, and still spent most of their time asleep, but they could move enough to see each other.

"Are they happy to have their sister home?" Violet asked and joined Keily and Rosa on the floor.

"They seem excited about it, yes," Keily replied with a glance at her sister. "I wasn't sure they'd notice, but since I've had them on the floor here all they seem to want to do is look at each other and hold hands."

Zinnia had Zoe's right hand in her left, while Zara's left hand was in her right. They were all wobbling and cooing at each other, sticking their tongues out and generally happy to be together, from the looks of it.

"It's like they knew something was missing," Keily observed out loud. "But now that missing puzzle piece is back and they're complete."

"I guess that is what happened, isn't it?" Rosa asked and wiped a little dribble of spit from Zoe's mouth. "She's still so little."

"I know, but they'll catch up eventually, I guess." Keily frowned. "I don't know, maybe they won't. But I think they will."

"Probably, as they get older." Violet picked up Zara when she started to frown and kick. "Somebody's about to need a new diaper."

"I think there's two that need changing." Rosa picked up Zoe, as gentle as everybody else that picked the baby up and stood with her. "But Aunty Rosa is here to help, right, my darling?"

Keily smiled and took Zinnia's hand when she continued to reach out for her sisters. "They'll be back in a minute, my love."

Zinnia cooed up at her mommy and Keily laughed. This had been a brutal experience, but one she wouldn't have given up for anything. Especially at times like now, when she got the most delighted cackle of sound from Zinnia. They really were precious moments, little videos burned into her memory that would never fade away.

The doorbell rang and Keily looked up from her daughter's face with confusion. They didn't get many visitors at Logan's, other than Rosa and Violet, so she was a little confused when the doorbell rang. "Logan will get it."

But Logan was soon at the nursery door, a frown on his face. "Um, Keily, Violet, it seems your parents are here?"

It was a question because he knew Keily hadn't invited them and never would. He looked at Violet, to see if she was responsible, but she was just as upset as Keily by the news.

"What the fuck are those two doing here?" Violet's face, dark and cloudy with anger, told Logan and Keily that she had nothing to do with their parents' sudden appearance. "Let me just go and tell them to fuck off back where they came from and I'll be back in a minute."

Violet stood up, handed Zara to Logan, but Keily stopped her.

"Let me come with you, Violet. We need to do this together, I think." Keily put Zinnia in her crib and took her sister's hand.

Violet looked over at Keily and saw just as much fierce determination on her sister's face as she felt. "We can do this."

"We can, together, Keily." Violet agreed and they walked down the steps.

"Girls, you both look so good!" Heather, their mother cried from the living room couch.

Keily and Violet had walked towards the door but obviously Logan had shown their parents in or, most likely, their mother had let herself in and made herself comfortable. While Heather pretended to not look around, ticking up prices with everything her eyes fell on, Keily glared at her father, Steve. He sat meekly on the couch, not looking at anything, not even moving. If it wasn't for the fact that she could see his chest move, Keily would have wondered if her father was dead.

Keily turned her eyes back to her mother, who was blathering on about their drive up from Florida, as if her hair wasn't thin and dirty, as if her teeth hadn't given up the fight long ago against the meth Heather loved so dearly, as if her skin and health weren't in the gutter from the same culprit.

Heather had lost so much weight her eyes appeared to be two huge marbles in the head of a skeleton, her lips and skin dry and flaky. Keily's upper lip pulled in a little as she looked her mother over, distaste, disgust, and pity mingling into one ball of whirling anger. How had her father allowed her mother to get this bad? Keily wondered as her mother all but bounced maniacally in place, like a clown on crack. Or maybe she was on crack, Keily wondered as her mother twirled in place, screeching about how proud she was of Keily.

"I always knew you'd make the big time, baby, and you have. Momma's so proud." Heather tried to hug Keily but Keily backed up, holding her mother off, and the smell of decay her mother gave off, with hands out to stop her.

"No. Just no. You left Violet on her own when she had Alice, you didn't even come to see her. Not to mention all the money you've stolen from me over the years. Nope, you don't get to do this. Dad." Keily paused but her dad didn't move a muscle. *"Dad!"*

Shouting the word at him seemed to break the stupor he was in. "Yes?"

"Get Mom and get the fuck out of here. Neither of you are wanted. Mom, you can destroy your own life if you want to, and Dad you can let her if you're that damn lazy, but you will not destroy mine or my children's." Keily spoke calmly, but inside she was shaking with anger.

"I'm with Keily, just go. I don't need your kind of pride, Mom, and a good thing, because you haven't ever given me an ounce of love. As Keily said, get the fuck out and don't come back. Don't come near me or my child, and don't ever, ever show up at my house. Ever." Violet, unlike Keily, walked closer, one finger held out in their mother's direction until the woman backed up against the front door. "Go and don't ever come back."

"But…" Heather looked around, her eyes full of greed and dollar signs. "But you have so much, Keily."

"I don't. This isn't my home. I live in a trailer on the other side of town." Keily paused as her mother's eyes fell to the ground in disappointment. "Oh, does that bother you, Mommy dearest? To know your beauty pageant queen daughter is now the proud renter of a trailer on the wrong side of town? Too fucking bad. Out!"

"But, honey, Joe told us you were doing great, that this was your house." Heather started but then looked over at Steve with eyes full of guilt.

"Ah, it's Joe. Joe told you. Great." Keily shook her head with annoyance. "Go on, get out before I call the police."

"It's not your house." Heather countered. "And those are *my* grandchildren up there. I have a right to see them."

"No, you don't. Not a single right." Keily pulled her phone from a pocket on her dress and started to dial the local police, still listed in her contacts from her run-ins with Joe in the past.

"Fine, fine, we'll go," Heather muttered something under her breath but Keily didn't care what the other woman had to say. "Come on, Steve."

"Y'all take care now, and have a nice drive back to Florida." Violet drawled with thick sarcasm. "Don't bother coming right on back. You aren't welcome here anymore."

Keily smiled over at her sister as she put her phone back in her pocket, proud of the young woman waving at their parents, now scurrying out of the door.

"I didn't know that would feel that good," Keily said to Violet whose eyes were shining with pleasure.

"Me either. But I'm glad I was here to do it with you, Keily." Violet answered and took her sister in her arms.

It was a nice place to be, wrapped up in her sister's arms, Keily decided. Even if the arms she wanted to be wrapped in were Logan's. Maybe someday. Maybe.

15

____

Logan

*L*ogan was lost in his office the next day. He wanted to spend time with the girls, but he had to handle problems at work that needed his attention. Financially, he could sell the whole business right now and have enough money for several lifetimes, but that wasn't what he ultimately wanted. He liked what he did, he liked employing people, and producing new and innovative self-defense products. Things would calm down now that Zoe was home with them, and maybe he'd find a way to balance all of this. After all, it was the age of technology.

Once the girls were older and more independent, he'd have little to fill his time with anyway, so he'd find someone to stand in as he'd done in California and cut back on the time he spent on work for now. They needed his attention right now, as did Keily. She was shaken by her mother's visit yesterday, although she seemed relieved at the same time.

She'd told him it was a final break with her past when he went in to visit her the night before.

"She took so much from me, Logan, not just money. My childhood, who I was, who I wanted to be, and did it all for a nasty habit that she won't get help for. It's better she's gone, for good I hope." Keily was on her bed, arms around her knees again, as if to protect herself from any harm her mother could cause, rather than relaxed as she'd been the last time he was in her room.

"That's all I need to know, then. You don't want her in your life, or the lives of our girls, that's fine with me." He didn't add that his own parents hadn't even bothered to email him back when he'd sent them one set of pictures. He'd stopped contacting them once he realized no reply was coming. There was no point in trying, they just didn't care and that was simply how it was.

"They have Rosa and Violet, as well as Avery and Judith. That's enough." Keily had forced a smile but the pain behind that smile still tugged at the strings of Logan's heart.

His thoughts were interrupted by the doorbell going off for a second day in a row. Even Rosa and Violet didn't ring the doorbell anymore. They knew they were welcome and just came in, usually straight up to the nursery. If it was that woman again…

He muttered under his breath about asshole parents and how he'd never be like that with his own daughters as he walked out of his office to answer the door. When he saw Keily's mother, dirtier than the day before, her hand clutching at the doorframe with dirty black finger-nails, Logan cringed.

"I will call the police if you do not leave, right now." He said, not realizing he was repeating Keily's words from the day before.

"I just wanted to talk to you. You're my baby's man, right?" Heather, that's what her name was, he remem-bered now, tried to elbow her way in past him but he stood firm.

"It doesn't matter if I'm her man or her gardener, madam, you aren't wanted here. You were told that yesterday." He glared down at her tiny frame, her gray eyes, Keily's eyes, haunted with insatiable need and full of hungry greed. Not Keily's eyes at all, he thought, these were the eyes of nothing but avarice.

"But listen, I just need a couple of thousand dollars, to get back to Florida you know? Keily broke my heart yesterday, you know, and I just need a little bit to get me by. I'll pay you back." The words rushed out of the dark-rimmed lips, probably a lack of oxygen, or damage from her drug habit, Logan noted without pity. This woman had made Keily the girl she was, had turned her into a snotty little snob, and had taken so much from her. He had no pity for her at all.

"No, leave." Logan nodded his head towards the cheap car outside the door and looked back at her dispassionately.

"But I never tried to hurt her, you know? I don't know what she's told you, but I made her who she was. I made her a queen." The woman stood a little straighter, but the weight of decades of drug abuse soon pulled her back into a slouch. "I made her who she was."

"I know, I remember how you turned a bright, charming, friendly young girl into a malicious, snotty, young woman that sneered at those she thought were beneath her. I saw how you pinched her at school assemblies, when she didn't want to strut and preen for an audience and only wanted to go home. I remember one particular incident where she threw up, because she was sick, and you slapped her and made her come out on the stage anyway. We all saw it, Heather. All of us, but you were so oblivious you didn't realize that. I know now you were probably too high to notice, but we did. So don't play innocent, proud mother with me. You're anything but. Now go, before I really lose my patience."

"But, man, I really need some cash!" Heather almost screeched, losing her patience. "That bitch owes me for all the money I spent on her."

"Oh, you mean the money you stole off of her? Let me tell you now, Heather, I know what you did. You will never, ever come near my daughters, you will never corrupt them, touch them, or anything else. I will not give you a dime and if you were never to contact us again, that would be awesome. So, I'll ask you once again, as politely as I can, to fuck off."

"Fuck you, whatever your name is. Logan, that's what Joe said it was. Fuck you, man, and fuck that bitch too." Her ugly face twisted and for a second Logan thought she was going to spit at him. She seemed to realize that would be the worst mistake she could make when she looked him in the eye.

"Nope, don't do that you ugly witch. Now, for the very last time, goodbye. And good riddance." Logan closed the door in her face and turned around to see Keily on the stairs. He started to speak, to apologize, but she just smiled with a nod and turned around to go back to the girls.

He decided he'd talk to her about it later, for now, she looked pleased and he'd leave it at that. He went back to his office to finish up the business tasks that needed his attention the most and then went into the nursery.

Keily was asleep on the couch with Zoe on her chest and Avery had Zinnia, rocking her back to sleep in a rocker. Logan went to Zara's crib and looked down at his daughter. She wasn't asleep and her eyes latched onto his. Something about the way she looked at him reminded him of something and then he remembered pictures of himself that he'd seen as a child. Maybe the girls did have some of their daddy in them after all.

"That's my girl." He said as he picked her up and put her against his shoulder. "How are you, sweet pea?"

He left the nursery with her and walked around the house, just walking to spend time with her in a room that wasn't the nursery. He found the housekeeper in the kitchen, happily making dinner for the adults in the house.

"Oh, can I hold her for a minute?" Judith held her hands out and Logan handed her over. "Which one is this?"

"Zara, the ever so serious one." Logan cooed at the baby as she blinked at him from Judith's arms. She was so serious, but then she broke the moment by sticking her entire hand in her mouth. "Maybe not always so serious."

"Maybe not, Logan. My goodness, they're all so beautiful, I have to say." Judith brushed the back of a finger down Zara's silky skin, pleased when Zara followed the finger. "I can't believe there's three of them."

"Believe me, there are three of them, and we know it when they all start crying at the same time. She'll start fussing soon too. She knows there are two sisters and if they're not close enough for too long, they kick up a huge fuss about it."

"Aw, that's sweet." Judith cooed before she handed Zara back to her father. "Thank you, but I have to get back to this sauce or it will burn."

"Any time, Judith. I'm going to take her back up to her sisters now." Logan snuggled Zara against his shoulder, his hand over her head, and went back up to see Keily awake and feeding Zinnia.

"She woke you up?" Logan asked and watched as Keily shifted the baby from one breast to the other.

"She woke us all up; Avery is feeding Zoe." Keily blinked and her eyes went out of focus for a minute. "I think I need more naps today."

"When she's finished you should go and lie down." He answered immediately, wanting her to have what she needed.

"I might just do that." She replied and leaned back, Zinnia still happily feeding away.

Her eyes came up to his for a second, a promise there, but then she looked down at the baby in her arms and the look vanished. Had that been desire he saw there? His heart thundered in his chest, but he turned away. Now wasn't the time, not when the babies needed her.

He left the room, scenarios playing in his mind as

he headed for the shower, a refuge for the last few weeks. He'd had so many fantasies about her in that shower, but he'd never tell her that. When he was feeling a little less stressed, Logan got out of the shower and put on a clean pair of black sweatpants and a black t-shirt.

By the time they'd had dinner and the world was dark once more, Logan's fantasies were back in his head. She'd looked at him the way she used to, before he broke her heart, over dinner, and there was hope at last. She was thawing towards him and it was showing. He was about to go to his room when she came out to the hallway, her hair damp on her shoulders, a thin cotton nightgown all that hid her nudity.

Yeah, that doesn't help, he thought as he glued his eyes to hers. If he stared at her breasts, she'd probably get offended. She'd just fed the babies and they weren't as round as they were before that final feeding of the evening, but they were still delectably firm and her nipples darker than they were before she got pregnant. The round nubs were clearly visible beneath the cotton, hard peaks that drew his gaze, no matter how hard he tried to look elsewhere.

"Logan?" She called out to him and he walked over to her when she leaned back against the wall. "Come in for a minute?"

"Sure." He answered and followed her like a lost

puppy. He didn't even blink when she closed the door and walked up to him, her fingers walking up his chest.

"Thanks for today. My mother, I mean." She looked up into his eyes, her eyes on his lips. "It meant a lot to me."

"You're welcome." He breathed out, instantly hard and ready for her but not willing to make a move, in case he scared her off.

She perched on her tiptoes and wrapped her arms around his neck. He forgot how to breathe as her soft lips found his and her breasts pressed into his chest. "I shouldn't do this, but I can't help myself."

The words were whispered against his lips before she pressed deeper and her tongue also pressed into him. His hands settled on her hips to hold her snugly against his body, where he wanted her, soft and giving in all the right places. His tongue came to meet hers and he inhaled the clean scent of her so close to him.

Desire flared into life, uncontrollable, unexpected, and all he could do was let her have whatever it was she wanted from him. Her right hand came down, slid beneath his shirt to the flat plane of his stomach, down to his hard cock, before she squeezed him ever so slightly.

Logan groaned into her mouth, ready to turn her around, push her against the bed, and fuck her, but he'd read about the operation she'd had, about the time it would take her to heal and how the surgery might affect her. He had to be gentle, when and if she initiated sex. This might not be the beginning of sex, no matter how much she wanted it. It might be a whimsy, or her hormones, or something else that would make her step away from him.

He'd let her lead, but while her hand was cupped over him, pressing into him in a hell located somewhere between pleasure and pain, he didn't really think all that much. He just enjoyed the soft feel of her breasts against him and the cherry taste of her tongue on his.

"Fuck, Keily, don't stop." He groaned when she pulled away enough to push the top of his pants down to grasp him fully. He thought he'd come in her hand, and he might have if he hadn't handled himself earlier in the shower.

"I'm not going anywhere." She whispered before she pressed her lips back to his.

Memories flooded into his mind, Keily on her knees, his cock down her throat, or beneath him in his bed, over him on that couch when they went on vacation all those many months ago. When the girls were old enough to not need them every moment of the day, he'd have to take her back to that island paradise, he decided.

"I want you, Logan." She whispered as she left his lips to kiss a trail down his neck.

She was about to drop to her knees, her lips already open for him when Avery knocked at the door.

"Keily, I'm sorry but Zinnia has a little fever. I thought you'd want to know."

All thoughts of sex and pleasure flew out of the window. Their daughter needed them.

"Sorry," Keily whispered as she stood back up and threw a robe on.

"No, it's fine. Zinnia needs us." Logan said, but he really wanted to shout obscenities as he took his hard cock in hand and pushed it back into his pants. He took deep breaths until it went down and then turned to open the door. He saw the indecision on her face as thoughts flickered around in her mind. He could actually see the moment she changed her mind about where she wanted this night to go.

Tension and frustration built inside until it almost ruptured, but he only allowed himself to clench his fists. Keily looked at him at last, the uncertainty still clear to see. She wanted him but for whatever reason, she was still holding back. All he could do was breathe in to calm himself down and let it go.

"Go on to bed, Logan, I'll see to her," Keily said as she left her room and headed for the nursery.

Not tonight then, he knew, but soon. Very soon, he hoped as he headed for the shower once more.

16

Keily

"They're three months old today. I can't believe it's only been twelve weeks. Everything has changed so much." Keily, in the nursery with her sister and best friend, looked down at little baby Zoe and felt her heart melt for the millionth time.

She'd been pregnant once before, far too soon to even know that she was pregnant really. It was another one of those things she'd forced herself to forget, mainly because the humiliation of Joe dropping his pants on live television for the entire viewing area to see had taken precedence. She remembered it now as she looked down into Zoe's face.

The pregnancy hadn't lasted long enough, hadn't been in her mind long enough for her to do anything other than mourn it as it ended. The same day she found out she was pregnant was the same day she lost the pregnancy. The same day her marriage ended.

Joe hadn't even known about the baby and probably wouldn't have until she started to show. Even if she'd told him, he drank so much back then that she knew he'd completely forget what she'd said the day before. The news wouldn't stick in his mind and that, even more than the humiliation he'd brought down on them both, was the real reason she'd left him. That was the day she knew, at last, that she could live without Joe, would be better off without him ruining everything.

It had been the right decision, whether she was now with Logan as his partner or not. She had three beautiful little girls to show for her decision, a home of her own, even if it was a trailer, and so much more. There was the relationship she now had with her sister, a female best friend that she adored, and pride in what she'd accomplished. Soon, she'd even get back into her classes and have a degree.

Yes, she thought as she stroked Zoe's cheek while the baby fed from a bottle, leaving Joe had been the best decision she'd ever made. "Sorry, I zoned out."

"It's alright, it must be easy to do when you have something so precious to look at, Keily," Rosa replied, her own arms filled with Zinnia.

"I can't believe they're my nieces." Violet breathed

with tears in her eyes, not for the first time. "You know I love Alice, I love her more than anything, but knowing these are your babies, Keily, that's just, damn, I'm sorry for getting all up in my feelings but they're just so precious."

"I get that now," Keily answered, her eyes on her sister's. "I was so caught up in my own pain and self-pity when Alice came along that I didn't get it then. I do now."

"It's about time," Violet said bluntly but tempered it with a smile and a wink. "My baby's awesome, you know?"

"She really is." Keily couldn't deny it. "Where is she?"

"I've started her at a Montessori day care," Violet said with pride. "It's costing me a fortune, but it's worth it."

"You'll have to explain what that is to me when it's time for the girls to start," Keily said and sat back in the rocker a little straighter. "Or is it something you start now?"

"It's just more educational than a regular daycare, they work with the children to start teaching them before other daycares would, and I guess it just depends on when you want to start them off with that sort of thing." Violet moved Zinnia around to rub her back.

"I don't want to part from them too soon, but I do need to get back to school and work eventually." Keily frowned, the thought of leaving the girls with someone she didn't know didn't bring happiness at all.

"You've got me, Keily." Avery reminded her and that brought a smile to Keily's face.

"I do, yes. Do you know this Montessori whatever?" Keily really had no idea what it was but if Violet wanted it for Alice, then it was probably something the girls should experience too.

"It was part of my childcare training, yes." Avery nodded and brushed red hair fading to gray behind her ears. "I've had a lot of training to qualify for this position and have a bachelor's degree in child development."

"Oh, I didn't know that." Keily blinked at the older woman. "I guess I just left it all up to Logan and assumed he'd make the best decision. It seems he did."

"Yes, the interview was very stringent, and I have to say, he'd done his homework because he knew all the right questions to ask me." Avery cleared her throat a little with a whisper of a smile on her face. "He was most professional."

"Good. Well, if you think you can handle all three then I guess I won't have to hunt down a daycare. Or Logan won't, that is." Keily felt bad that she'd never thought to ask Avery anything about her life and decided she would, later, when Rosa and Violet left.

"How's Zara doing over there, Rosa?" Keily darted her eyes over to see Rosa seemed relaxed, but there was tension around her eyes and in the set of her mouth. Her mouth always flattened out when she was thinking about something that upset her, Keily had learned. "What's wrong?"

"Just a little trouble in paradise." Rosa dismissed her own problems and cleared her face before she looked up at Keily. "Nothing to worry about."

"You're my BFF, Rosa, of course I'm worried." Keily stood up to go and sit on the floor with Zoe in her arms. "What's wrong?"

"Just a disagreement about vacation plans and things like that," Rosa sighed. "I don't want to go to Mexico. I've been. It's hot. I want to go somewhere cool, before the weather turns South Carolina into a humid oven." She rolled her eyes and looked down at her friend. "Does that make sense?"

"It does. But compromise is important." Keily said thoughtfully, remembering her marriage and how she'd always been the one to compromise. "Just so long as you aren't always the one giving in. It has to be fair."

"You're right. I can take a vacation on my own to somewhere cooler, later in the summer."

"Logan will give you more time off if you need it." Keily volunteered, knowing she'd glare him into submission if she had to do it. She'd do anything for her best friend.

"I love how much you two love each other. I never

thought I'd see the day when you had a best friend, Keily. And a female best friend at that." Violet stared at them in awe, her eyes big and round.

"It's gross isn't it?" Keily asked in a stage-whisper. "I mean, women are horrible creatures."

"And they're always trying to butt in," Rosa responded immediately.

"Always trying to outdo each other." Keily went on but leaned her head towards Rosa, as if to draw her closer.

"Women are horrible creatures," Rosa repeated and put one hand out to stroke Keily's hair before she put the hand back on Zara's head.

"You two are silly," Violet answered them both, but she couldn't hide how pleased she was. "Anyway, I have to get to work, so I'm off."

"You're on evening shifts again?" Keily frowned, knowing her sister hated that shift.

"Yes, and it's killing me, but it's only for this week. That's another good thing about Alice's daycare, they work with our schedules. I would be out of luck if it wasn't for that." Violet handed Zinnia off to Avery and stroked her face before she turned away. "I'll see you two tomorrow?"

"You will." Keily agreed and looked over at Rosa who nodded in agreement. Keily wasn't sure if Rosa and Violet were close but they did seem to get along well.

"See you then." Violet left with a wave and Avery followed her to leave for an appointment she had.

"We're alone at last," Rosa whispered with a grin.

"I know." Keily waggled her eyebrows and stood up to put Zoe in her crib. "Are you going to tell me about what's wrong or are you going to make me talk about myself?"

"I think your problems are bigger than mine, don't you?" Rosa continued to rock Zinnia, content to talk about Keily and her life. Keily got the hint that Rosa didn't want to talk about her own problems and let it go.

"I think I'm going to give Logan another chance. I know he broke my heart, before you say anything, but I can't ask people to accept that I've changed if I don't give Logan that same chance. I'm not the Keily that walked into his office all those months ago. I'm a totally different person now. And I think he is too."

"I think you're right." Rosa conceded after a moment's hesitation. "I've seen him with the babies, and you, and how he is at the office now, for that matter. When he's there."

"That's something else, isn't it? He spends more time here than he does at the office." Keily made the point and then went quiet. She wanted to know what Rosa thought.

"I think parenthood has made you both see the world differently. If you're both on the same page about things, then I guess it's not a bad idea to give it a chance. It's obvious he cares about you." She paused, her eyes on the wall beyond her before she looked back up at Keily. "I just don't want to see you broken like you were before ever again. I worry about that."

"I know, I do too, *but* I don't think it will happen again. He's so…different. He even talks now. He never really did that before." Keily knew the house was empty now except for her, the babies, and Rosa, and the babies weren't talking so it was safe for her to discuss these things. "He's not an open book like I am with you, but he's trying."

"Then it sounds like he really wants a relationship and not whatever the hell you were before." Rosa nodded in satisfaction. "It sounds like maybe you have a chance at real happiness, Keily, you should take that chance."

"I hope so. I don't want to fail the girls, or him, or me. I just want what everyone else seems to have so easily."

"I don't think it's as easy as it looks." Rosa contradicted her. "I think people just hide how hard they work at it. Or hide the fact that one is giving up more than the other. It's supposed to be a two-way street, this relationship stuff, but it's still hard to navigate."

"Especially when there's three streets, I guess?" Keily

broached the subject Rosa seemed most intent on avoiding.

"Grrr," Rosa growled at her, but gave in. "It's just a bump in the road, to continue the traffic euphemisms. As I said earlier, they want Mexico, I don't. There's also the fact that they don't seem to get that my family is from there and why I'm here, why I was born here. Why my family left Mexico to begin with."

"Oh, there's a whole lot more there than you were letting on?" Keily said with a lifted eyebrow. "Are you saying they don't respect who you are?"

"Kind of." Rose cringed and then frowned. "Not really, but sometimes, I think they forget I'm different to them."

"I see." Keily knew she was probably guilty of the same thing but had to use what she knew to help Rosa. "Maybe you need to tell them that? Not bite their heads off or anything, but maybe just kind of be yourself and tell them that shit's not cool?"

"Maybe." She looked doubtful. "You're probably right."

"I probably am. I'm not saying they're right, but maybe give them the benefit of the doubt?"

"Yeah, you're probably right. And don't think I didn't notice how *you* changed the subject this time." Rosa tsked at her friend and got up. "I have to go, my couple are both off this weekend and I need to get ready for a grownup talk, don't I?"

"Or you could stay and tell me more of your exploits?" Keily stood, a hopeful look plastered on her face, but Rosa shook her head.

"No more stories for you until you've got new stories of your own, woman." Rosa bared her straight teeth at her friend then smiled. "Good luck with whatever you decide."

"Thanks, I think I'll need it." Keily shrugged and followed her friend to the door. "See you next time."

"Probably tomorrow, but maybe later tomorrow?" Rosa made it a question, in case Keily had plans.

"I'll be here. I'm always here. At least until the girls get big enough to go outside when it's warmer."

"Good grief, if it gets any warmer, they'll bake out there."

"I'll have Logan hook up an air conditioner out there for us." Keily laughed but the smile faded as Rosa left with a wave.

She'd tried to get Logan to come back to her bed not long ago, had made it obvious what she'd wanted, but Zinnia had a fever that worried Avery and the nanny interrupted her attempt at seduction. Keily was up most of the night checking on all the babies after that and she'd sent Logan to bed, alone.

Sex was all but a distant memory for her but now

that her body was healed from the pregnancy, birth, and emergency surgery, she was coming back to life. Even the sex dreams had started back up and those didn't help when she lived with the most attractive man she'd ever laid eyes on. A man that slept feet away from her, only a few torturous feet away. So close, she could touch him, if she was brave enough. It was hard to be brave after what they'd been through.

After all, he'd walked out on her for a reason. Had he really forgiven her, or would that crop up again later, when she least expected it? After she'd put her heart and soul into a relationship he'd just walk away from it again?

Hours later her phone buzzed, breaking her train of thought. It was Logan's PA. Why was she calling?

"Hi, Keily? I'm sorry to disturb you. I know the hospital probably won't call you, so I am." The woman said, immediately causing Keily's stomach and heart to lurch into hard knots.

"Excuse me? What's going on?" Keily forced out from taut vocal cords.

"There's been an accident."

Keily's fingers went slack and the phone fell to the floor.

17

Logan

Logan didn't usually spend his Saturdays at the office, but he needed to be there to accept a package that should have come the day before, when his PA could have taken control of it. He got some work done until the package came. He decided to go and inspect the factory in the building next door before he left since it had been a while since he'd walked through there.

He noted a few safety hazards that he'd leave a note about and saw the weekend crew were having problems with one of the machines. He called in the repair crew and spent the rest of the day helping to get the machine up and running again. He wasn't above getting dirty with his employees and it felt good to do something with his hands again.

It was getting late, well after 7 pm, when Logan found himself deep in the guts of a machine that made the plastic parts for a small, but very useful, taser disguised as a phone case. The material they used in the injection molding machine was stuck in a roller that had malfunctioned and Logan was trying to lift one of the rollers with a crowbar while one of his employees fished around to retrieve the material. He'd learned long ago that the unbelievable happened when it came to large-scale production and today was one of those days.

His arms were straining as the load of the huge roller pulled at his muscles, and Logan wanted to tell Will, his employee, to get a move on, but he knew this had to be done right or they'd have to do it all again when they started the machine back up. Logan moved as the load became heavier, his grip on the crowbar slipping when his hands started to sweat and burn against the crow-bar's pull on his skin.

"Will, watch out!" Logan cried as he felt his grip slip completely, the crowbar pulling right out of his hands.

Will darted backward, knocking right into Logan as he did so. Logan felt time slow to an impossible crawl as he teetered backward, reached for the guard rail that surrounded the huge machine, but missed it. The world narrowed down to little more than the ceiling of his factory as he fell over the guard rails, the shouting voices of his employees a mumble of sound that made no sense. He knew what was coming next - impact - but he didn't think about that in the milliseconds before he hit the concrete floor, he thought of Keily and their girls.

Pain exploded in his left leg, his left hip, along his right shoulder, and finally in his head. He felt the bones splinter in his leg and was certain he heard the loudest sound he'd ever heard as his skull cracked when his head bounced on the floor. That's when the world went instantly black for Logan.

"START AN IV DRIP...YOU got his leg stabilized? Right, let's move him." Logan heard female voices from somewhere in the darkness he now inhabited. He perceived movement but had no idea where he was going or how he was getting there.

"Keily..." He mumbled, reaching for her, but she wasn't there.

The world went dark and silent again.

"What's wrong with him, why won't he wake up?" He heard Keily's voice demand, and he wondered who she was talking about and why she sounded so panicked and angry.

The world faded away again.

"We've repaired the damage to his leg." He heard someone say but he couldn't ask whose leg was damaged or why they were telling him about the guy's leg. It wasn't any of his business, but he couldn't move his lips or make his throat work.

What was going on? Why couldn't he speak? Or move?

The darkness tugged at him again, invited him to escape this strange place and he accepted, for now.

Time passed slowly, too quickly, in uncountable seconds for Logan. There were moments of near awareness when he caught snippets of sentences, a flash of sunlight, the smell of food, but he could not seem to pull himself out of the darkness. Was this what Keily felt after her surgery, something she'd tried to explain to him a few times? He felt as if he was drowning in the darkness, trapped there and unable to escape. He clawed at the darkness, looking for a foothold, for a way to tear himself free or climb out of this black hell, but nothing happened. He remained alone, without the woman he…loved.

The thought, all thoughts, floated away and he knew nothing for a while.

A streak of sunlight seared the crack in his eyelids before it disappeared. Too bright, too painful. Go back to the dark.

At other times there was pain, but it only lasted for a few moments before it flowed away into a black river that blended into the world he now inhabited. Logan floated there, suspended in nothing, his thoughts coming to life every now and then, bringing him back to something like reality, if reality was a black echoing cave.

He had no concept of time, had no idea how long he'd been in that strange world, but he knew he wanted to escape it. He wanted to be at home with his girls, with Keily. His family. The only real thing that mattered to him.

Maybe he'd lost his chance, maybe this was really Hell and he'd never escape, he worried, on the occasions when he could think of anything at all. What if this was it? What if he'd…died?

This couldn't be it, though. Life had been so cruel to him until he stopped waiting for the world to be nice to him and took his fate into his own hands. He'd made something for himself and when the chance came to have far more than he'd ever hoped to have, he'd taken it. Hadn't he?

18

Keily

She rushed to the hospital within minutes of Avery coming in to check on her. There'd been a sound, something like a wounded animal in the last mortal throes of a very painful death, a sound Keily hadn't understood came from her, until Avery rushed in to help. Logan was in the hospital, he'd fallen off one of the machines, a 15-foot drop. He had a head injury.

Keily didn't know how bad the injury was but her brain produced a million horrifying images as she raced to the hospital he'd been taken to. As a stop light held her up, seeming to take much longer than it normally did, Keily imagined him dying without her there for his last moments, without having ever heard her say that she loved him. Had she missed her chance?

Rosa and Violet both called her as she drove but Keily didn't answer. She was barely aware that she was driving now, in too much of a panic to be completely aware but still understanding that even the hands-free distraction might be too much for her to deal with at the moment. She had to get to the hospital, had to know what was wrong, had to know if Logan was still…alive.

Tears streamed unchecked down her face, and she was totally unaware of the way sobs tore from her throat. All she cared about was following the road to the hospital and once she was there, finding a spot to park. She could just leave the car at the emergency room entrance, but she knew it would get towed, and it wasn't really a nice thing to do.

She scoffed out a smile through the watery mess of her face. A year ago, she'd have parked there anyway. Logan had changed her entirely, even down to that little nicety. Would he be there to see how she changed in the future? To see how their girls changed and grew over the years?

He had to be.

The words became a mantra as she walked into the emergency department and asked to know where Logan was. She explained that she was Logan's girlfriend, that she had three baby girls at home that wanted to have their daddy back, and the woman at the reception area gave in and finally told Keily where he was.

When she made it back to the private room where Logan was being cared for Keily looked around, expecting to see rushing medical staff, but there was nothing. Keily hesitated in the door, looking around in confusion. Was this the wrong room?

"Can I help you?" A male nurse walked by and stopped when he saw Keily was in a bit of a predicament.

"Is this Logan Sinclair's room?" Keily waved her right hand in the direction of the room.

"Oh yes, he's down in surgery. Are you a relative?" The nurse's face changed, became concerned.

"I'm his girlfriend." Keily wondered if she should lie, tell them she was his fiancée or something, but decided against it.

"Okay. Well, he's got a fractured leg and a serious head injury. They're operating now. You can wait here and I'll update you if I hear anything."

"Oh god." Keily gasped, her heart pounding. She felt like sinking down to the floor but held herself together enough to stand on her shaky legs and squeeze out a question. "Is he... alright?"

"He was unconscious when they brought him in and the doctors were concerned about a bleed in his brain, so he went straight into the OR after his scans. The doctors are hopeful he'll make a good recovery but we'll know more when they're out." The man, probably in his late thirties if the lines around his eyes meant anything, spoke low and soft, as if he were afraid Keily was about to collapse.

Keily stood firm now though, knowing she had to be strong for her daughters and for Logan. She'd get through this, and so would he. He'd fight to come back for the girls, and for her. He deserved a happy life and she promised herself that when he managed to get through this, she'd spend every day making sure he had a reason to smile.

Logan didn't wake up that first night, but Keily held firm through every day. Every morning she shaved his face because she knew he hated to not be clean-shaven, and she told him about all the things they would do together and with the girls. At the end of every night, she ignored Rosa's and Violet's pleas to go home and rest.

Logan needed her. The girls did too, of course, but Logan had nobody to look after him. The girls had Avery, Violet, and Rosa, and her when they were at the hospital with her. She felt a pang of guilt over it all, but she was terrified to leave his side. What if he…woke up and she wasn't there?

She refused to think of any other possibility, even in silent meditation, her thoughts locked away from everyone around her. Even in the most private place of all, she refused to allow herself to think that anything else would happen. Logan *would* wake up. It was only a matter of when.

The doctor reassured her that Logan would wake up when he was ready. It wasn't uncommon for patients to stay in a coma for a while after a serious brain injury. If all went well, she'd see his gorgeous brown eyes again without having to peel his eyelids open, she'd feel his warm dry lips pressing back against hers as he took her in his arms.

"You have to come back to me, Logan." She said a week after his accident, as the second week of coma started. "You have to come back so I can tell you I love you. So, you can watch the girls grow up. So, we can grow old together."

She laid her head against his on the pillow and clasped his hand in hers. For a second, she thought he squeezed back, but the moment passed. "Please, Logan. Don't leave me alone like this."

19

Logan

In that void of nothing, Logan wondered if there was something more he could have done. He knew then that he should have told Keily he loved her, should have asked her to be his wife, should have made more of an effort to push her, even if it had made sense not to. She needed that space he gave her, needed to adjust to being a mother and a woman who would never have more children than the three that she had. But she'd needed him too, hadn't she?

Logan wanted a chance to tell her that he not only loved their children, really loved them in a way he'd never expected, but he loved her too. He concentrated when he could, worked on finding a way out of this infernal nothingness, tried to let the voices he heard draw him back to where those voices lived. He couldn't scream or break anything in this place, but he was certain he nearly broke his own mind trying to escape it.

He had to get back to Keily, no matter what it took. He had to tell her...

"I love you." The words whispered from dry lips as he opened his eyes and found himself in a very unfamiliar place.

"Did you say something, Mr. Sinclair?" He heard a voice ask.

"Where am I?" His dry throat barely squeaked the words out but they did come out.

"You're in hospital. You had an accident and you've been in a coma. We were just running some scans to check on your recovery." The disembodied voice said mechanically. "Mr. Sinclair, can you hear me?"

"Keily." He whispered, wanting her there with him, needing her there to make the confusion go away. She was the only one that could make the world make sense.

He looked around with just his eyes, so used to not being able to move that it didn't occur to him to try to turn his head yet. He heard loud pulsing sounds and seemed to be lying in a small white tunnel. An MRI?

"Please don't move, Mr. Sinclair." The voice spoke from somewhere above him, through a speaker perhaps?

Logan blinked his eyes, realized his head was strapped

down and that his body didn't feel like his own. He wanted to ignore the voice, to explore the white panels that surrounded him, to get out of the machine, to find…Keily.

"My wife…er, no." Logan paused. That was wrong. Keily wasn't his wife, but he desperately wanted her to be. She should be his wife. "Keily?"

"She's upstairs waiting for you, Mr. Sinclair. Now, please, relax and don't move." The technician relieved Logan by saying.

"What's wrong with me?" He couldn't really *feel* any part of his body, everything was numb. They must have given him drugs.

"You've been in an accident. I won't know the extent of your injuries until I've finished the tests."

Logan relaxed finally and stopped fidgeting. The room was cool and he wanted a blanket, something that would fight off the chill he felt. He kept it all to himself and smiled up gratefully at the man and woman that came to move him back to a gurney before the man pushed him back to his room on the second floor of the hospital.

"Is he awake?" He heard Keily ask and looked over at her. Her face was pinched with worry and her makeup was in a mess but that didn't matter. She was one of the most beautiful sights he'd ever seen.

"Awake and fidgeting." The man said with a quiet

laugh. "I think he's going to be awake for a while this time.

Logan smiled over at Keily while a nurse and the man from radiology moved him back to his bed. He looked down to see a temporary brace on his leg and that his clothes had been replaced by a hospital gown. "I take it I didn't show the floor who's boss?"

"Fuck me, no, you didn't Logan," Keily whispered when she'd taken a seat on the side of his bed. She grabbed his hands up in hers to kiss them. "What happened? Do you remember?"

"The crowbar slipped, and Will jumped back." Logan stopped as the memory replayed. Exhaustion pulled at him, but she was real, he could smell her perfume, feel her skin, knew she was real, and he didn't want to ever leave her again.

"I was so afraid when I got the call from the factory. They told me you were bleeding from your head, that you'd fallen over fifteen feet…" Her voice trailed off. Her eyes were shiny with unshed tears, and a sob broke free of her throat. "I thought, after all that we'd been through with the girls that we'd get a break for a while, but that all changed. I was picturing you as they described you, broken, bleeding, worse."

"I'm here, Keily," Logan whispered, his throat suspiciously tight after the fear she'd poured out. He didn't want to leave her, not ever again, and especially not forever. "I'm not leaving."

"You certainly aren't, Mr. Sinclair." A female voice intruded into their private moment, full of cheer and wisdom. "You have a brain injury, a fractured leg, some bruising that is healing, a few muscle tears that are also healing, but we're confident that you'll recover. You've been in a coma, but hopefully, that's over now."

"How long?" He asked, his voice raspy. Keily moved to bring a cup filled with ice water to his lips and he took a long drink through a straw.

"Two weeks now," Keily answered for the nurse. "Two very long weeks."

He sighed when she put the cup down to stroke his face. He didn't feel a beard so someone must have shaved him. It was an odd thing to think about, knowing someone had shaved his face without him being even slightly aware of it.

He looked up at her and wanted to share everything he'd thought about while he was 'gone' but…lethargy took over.

"You'll be sleepy from the pain medicine, Mr. Sinclair." The nurse warned and Logan wanted to tear the IV out of his arm…or wherever they'd put the drip. His body still didn't feel completely like it was his own.

Sleep took him before he could say anything else,

before he could reveal everything to Keily, but this was natural sleep. The kind that came with dreams unplagued by fear or nightmares. He'd wake up at some point, he'd get that chance he'd been terrified he'd lost. He hoped.

When he woke up again the room was lit only by the screens of the many machines he was hooked up to. He was…alone.

Had it all been a dream, he wondered as he looked around but didn't see signs of life anywhere. Had he been hurt in California when the earthquake struck there? Fear clenched at his heart as that thought took hold and sunk roots into his brain. Were the babies real? The struggle that poor Keily had been through, was that all a part of a nightmare? He searched the room for any signs of what could be, had been, would be, but saw nothing but medical equipment, a TV, and a large window.

Where was he?

He looked around, saw a whiteboard with the names of his nurses, and a graphic that read 'Mercy Emergency Hospital of King's Hill'. Okay, he knew where he was now, even if the hospital had a strange name. Logan took a deep breath and looked around his bed. He wasn't often sick, rarely needed a doctor, but he'd visited people a few times and knew there should be a call button on his bed somewhere.

He pushed the button, and a loud voice made his eyes go wide in shock. "Is that you, Mr. Sinclair?"

"Yes, can someone tell me what's going on?"

"I'll be right in, Mr. Sinclair." The matronly female voice responded and Logan sat back. Impatience nagged at him as he waited for the nurse to come in to see him, but he reminded himself that the woman probably had a lot to do.

"I sent that pretty little thing that's been by your side the last two weeks home just a little while ago, Mr. Sinclair." A woman in her mid-50s said as she walked into the room patting dark gray hair into place. "She's wearing herself out watching over you and those adorable babies of yours."

"Keily?" He asked, hope blossoming into life again.

"Yes, such a pretty name. She'll be back soon, I'm sure. Now, let's have a look at that IV, shall we?" She asked with a friendly smile that put him at ease.

It didn't matter what she wanted to check, or if she wanted him to run naked through the hallways. He was in South Carolina and everything he remembered was real. Most importantly, he was truly awake, at last. "Is there anything to eat at this time of night?"

"We'll find you something, honey." The nurse patted his arm and Logan smiled. This was good. Very good.

20

Logan

A week later Logan put down the telephone in his office and almost wished he was still in the hospital. Keily had banned his phone the first full week he was awake, and life had been rather peaceful, even when Rosa and Violet brought in his baby girls to see him. He was released from the hospital after that and today was the first day he'd ventured out on his crutches.

"Sorry about that." He said as Keily came into his home office, her eyebrows knitted together in a death glare. "I missed dinner, I know. One of the machines broke down and I ended up having to call in the repair crew to fix it. And the main supervisor I told you about, the one I'm getting all the complaints about who had left all those safety hazards unrepaired the day I got hurt? He's now fired."

"I don't blame you," Keily answered succinctly. Logan didn't fire employees over nothing. He gave them a chance to improve and if they didn't, he gave them the boot. The guy wasn't to blame for Logan's accident, but someone else could have been hurt because of the supervisor's lax standards.

"There were safety hazards all over the place." Logan continued, going over it all again in his head. "I fixed what I could, but some of it needed to be blocked off until a repair crew can fix it. Anyway, that guy is gone."

It was nice just to talk to her and get this stuff off of his chest. That was one of the nice things about their relationship, they actually talked about their day together, discussed problems, and worked together to fix them. Yeah, he missed the fuck out of sex with her, but talking was important, he'd come to learn. It helped to relieve some of the stress he felt, and he slept better at night.

Especially since she'd seemed to conquer those nightmares of his and he'd managed to climb his way out of a coma. The nightmares hadn't woken him up since that night she slipped into bed and cradled him until he went back to sleep or since he woke up from his coma. He almost worried he was in for another year of torment after the nightmare of that coma but something about her seemed to have vanquished the kid in him that was still afraid of being attacked.

"He definitely deserves to be fired then. He knows people are there on the weekends, even if he's off at the lake or whatever it is he does. He's always going on about fishing." He heard Keily say with irritation. "I didn't like the guy either when I was working there, I have to say."

"No, you didn't." Logan agreed and nodded, his leg up on a chair in a soft brace to protect it. The break hadn't been that bad and he barely felt any pain in it at all now. "Are the girls asleep?"

It was dark already, so they probably were.

"Yes, Zoe just went off at last. I didn't think she was going to stop fighting her sleep, but she did."

"Okay. Want to watch a movie together or something?" Logan held his breath as he waited for her answer. It had been a while since they'd had time to themselves, alone, watching movies like they used to. Maybe he'd get a chance to work up the nerve to say all the things he'd promised himself he'd say.

"Yeah, we can watch it in my room if you want? That way we can hear the girls if they need us." Logan wasn't sure but he thought he heard a note of hope in her voice too, as if she really wanted him to say yes and not just because of the girls.

"Let Avery do her job, Keily. Relax for a change." He urged her, even though he knew she wouldn't listen.

"I know, I just worry so much about them." She let the words trail off.

"And I understand that, but they're fine, honey. They're okay. And we'll be right there."

"I know. You're right." She didn't say anything else, so he let her off the hook and dropped the subject.

"I'll join you in about ten minutes. I have one more phone call to make. Want to pick something out and I'll join you in your room?"

"Sounds good. I'll see if Judith is around to heat up something for you to eat, too."

"No, that's alright. I'm good on that front."

"Oh, good. Okay. I'll see you in a little while then."

"You will, Keily." He picked up the phone and focused on getting the call over with as quickly as possible.

By the time he joined her in her bedroom, she was dressed in a white cotton nightgown and a cotton robe with hibiscus flowers decorating it. It was something he'd bought her when they went on vacation together and did little to calm the tension that came to life the moment he walked in the door. The robe, the memories of that vacation just made him more tense, in fact.

"Hey, how are you doing with those?" Keily asked as soon as he came in on his crutches.

"I'm fine, just tired." He had on gray pajama pants and a t-shirt, but wished he'd put on jeans that morning, they might have hidden how much he wanted her.

He rushed to sit down on the couch, hoping she hadn't seen. He knew her body was ready for sex, but was her mind? She'd left him hanging not long ago, backed away from him like he was the worst mistake she'd ever made. Yet here he was, about to watch a movie in her bedroom. He'd behave, until and unless she made a move of her own.

"It's been a long week. It'll do you some good to relax for a little while." She replied and turned the large flatscreen on to start the movie she'd chosen.

Logan kept his eyes on the TV, wanting to not be obvious about where his mind was. When he looked back over at her she'd pulled a blanket off the bed and had it wrapped around her feet. "You've got cold feet?"

"Not about watching the movie, no. Oh, you mean the blanket? Yeah, I should probably put some socks on, but I like having a blanket." She bit at her bottom lip and looked up at him, almost as if she felt guilty. "Do you really want to watch a movie, Logan?"

His heart thudded to a stop before it raced back into life, awareness almost electric between them.

"I want to do whatever you want to do, Keily." Instinct told him to shut up and do what he wanted to do, take what he wanted to take, say what he wanted to say but he held back, gave her some space. "What do you want to do?"

"I think I want to do something else, Logan. I just have to know it'll be different this time. That you won't run out on me, even if the reason you did was my own fault." She looked up at him with pain and desire in her eyes.

"I only needed you to say the word, Keily." He breathed in relief. Whatever happened, they were talking at least.

He looked over at her and found himself spellbound by her. Her eyes, always so captivating, held him as he looked at her, drew him in, but they needed to talk first. Kissing could come later. For now, his beautiful, brave, and oh so strong Keily needed to know that he would always be there for her.

"I didn't know what life was until I met you, Keily. Well, until I met you as an adult." He laughed at the awkwardness of the situation, at himself. He had to laugh again when he struggled up off the couch and hobbled over to sit on the bed with her. "I thought I knew what life was, but you brought laughter into my world, joy, and so many other things. I was still too caught up in my anger from the past to be what you needed me to be. I was still caught up in who you had been to see what you were giving to me. I knew what I'd lost the minute I left your apartment that night, which is why I kept going back to it, even after you were gone. I wanted back what you'd given me, only I couldn't have it. Not until I saw you again. Not until you let me back into your life and I promise you, I don't ever plan to let that go."

"That's all I needed to know." She leaned into him. "We've both changed, grown up, I guess, and I really don't want to spend another second of my life without you. You gave me our daughters, but all I wanted when you left, was you. That hasn't changed. I still want you and only you, Logan. I almost lost you, or it felt like I did, when you had that accident. Don't make me live without you anymore."

Rather than answering her verbally, he took her lips suddenly, too hungry to hold back, to be gentle, if only for that second. Her tongue darted out to wet his lips, telling him to take what he wanted, to hurry because she couldn't take waiting any more than he could.

He told himself to go slow, to take it easy but Keily took that decision away from him when she pushed herself up and straddled his waist, their lips still sealed together. It had been so long since they'd kissed that Logan didn't want to let her lips go and gently held her face to his as she moved.

He wanted to pull away, to tell her to slow down, that they had the rest of their lives but he didn't want to break the connection, didn't want to risk missing that chance he'd silently screamed for while he was in the coma. As soon as her lips touched his, he came to life again in a way he hadn't realized was gone. The girls had brought something to him, given him a new purpose, but their mother? Now she gave him life unlike anything he'd ever felt before.

Eager hands brushed the robe from her shoulders as her tongue slid along his and the heat built between them, where their bodies met. He laughed deep in his throat when she groaned, not out of self-satisfied amusement but because he was so pleased she was in his arms. His hands slid up the nightgown bunched at her hips, gliding with satisfied delight over the silky expanse of her skin. She felt like home.

Where he was always supposed to be, where he should have been all those long empty months, here with her and nowhere else. But now wasn't the time for regret, it was time to build new memories, to create new tomorrows, and he would make that all come true, as long as she let him.

Their bodies pressed together intimately, and it was no surprise when he felt his chest grow damp. He'd read about it, knew what to expect, that her milk might leak, knew that other things about her might be different but it was all hot to him. She was excited and her body, always so responsive, told him exactly what she was feeling. She tried to pull away, embarrassed when she realized how wet they both were.

"No, Keily. It's you, it's part of you until you wean the girls and we'll just have to learn to enjoy it won't we?" He told her, his fingers reaching out to stroke her nipples, coaxing them into life. There wasn't much left in her, not after feeding the girls, so all he got for his troubles were tight peaks that needed to be touched.

He slid the nightgown over her head until she was bare, naked to his gaze. "Let me taste you, it's been too long."

She looked down at him, uncertain, her need to ravish him gone as her body betrayed just how human she was. "If you want to. But don't do it just to make me feel better."

"I would never lie to you like that, Keily." He answered and took her breasts in his hand. Their shape was slightly different, her whole body was, but she'd exercised daily the last couple of months and was getting back some of her old shape. He liked her softer, rounder in places, but he'd never make her choose which way to be.

Besides, all he wanted at the moment was her nipple on his tongue. Keily breathed harshly as his tongue swept over her nipples, one at a time. When he pressed her breasts together and sucked, she pushed her hips down into his and groaned loudly, lost in the sensation.

He felt her hips begin to move on the hard ridge hidden in his pants and though it was a little uncomfortable at first, it had been so long since she'd touched him that it started to feel good. He let her do as she pleased, so long as she let him tease her tight nipples. He sucked them in long pulls, used his teeth to hold them for the lashing his tongue gave them, and teased sounds out of her that he loved. Soon she was panting while she danced on his cock.

"I need you, Logan, I need you so much. Fuck, I need you." She groaned almost to herself before she reached between their bodies, shifting just enough to let his length escape his pants before she slid down on him.

That pulled a groan from somewhere deep in his chest as he felt her walls enclose him, hot and wet, and all for him. "Keily."

Her name was a ragged whisper that he repeated as she began to move on him, fast and hard, harder than he thought she should move, but she insisted when he tried to hold her still, pushed down against his hold, until he let go and let her have her way. She knew what was best.

"Fuck, this is so good." She panted, her face a picture of lost rapture. "And the best part is, I don't have to worry about whether I'm going to get pregnant."

"That's definitely a bonus." He whispered, but wondered if it would bother her.

She didn't seem to care and he knew she mustn't

when he felt her contract around him, a tight grip like a slick fist around his cock. For a second she hung there, mouth open, eyes wide, until the pleasure broke over her, a tidal wave that washed away all that had come before. There was only them, now, and the future.

Logan couldn't help it, he followed with her as her nails dug into his shoulders and his cries mingled with hers. She was his again, at last. Nothing else mattered.

21

Logan

They're five months old today, Logan thought as he glanced at the girls in the back seat of the rental car they'd picked up at the airport. Five months and growing like weeds, he thought with pride as he turned into the driveway the navigation system pronounced was the address he wanted.

"The keys are supposed to be in the mailbox," Logan said to Keily and she jumped out of the car to walk to the mailbox in front of the gate. Luckily, it was his left leg he'd broken so he could still drive.

He looked over her frame with hungry eyes, always hungry, even after a month of having her every way he wanted her. He knew from past experience that it was unlikely he'd ever have enough of her. He smiled when she opened the gate with a comical bow and flourish to wave him in.

She closed the gate while he pulled the car up to the mansion he'd rented for the week in Puerto Rico. It had been a bit of a juggle to get the girl's passports in time, but he'd managed it. A quick glance up at the house revealed three stories in a traditional Spanish style with a terracotta roof and white adobe walls. Balconies ringed the top two floors and he knew the roof hid a terrace. Out back there was a pool, tennis courts, and an orange grove that filled the air with the sweet scent of orange blossoms.

"This is lovely, Logan," Avery said as she climbed out of the car and started to unbuckle the girls. "Just right, I should think."

Her eyes held a twinkle of knowledge that made him wonder if she'd guessed why he'd brought them here. It was a surprise, this trip, planned for many months now. When he started to plan it, he hadn't known exactly what he had in mind, other than a vacation for a woman that had just been through hell, but now he knew.

He touched his pocket, felt the small box there, and sighed. He hadn't lost the ring then. "I say we check what's inside, unload the girls, and head to the beach."

"I'll go to the grocery store if I need to." Avery volunteered as she pulled one car seat out and got out of the way.

By the time the girls were unloaded and the car unpacked it was mid-afternoon. Avery had rushed off to a supermarket down the street and was back in time for them all to go to the beach together. Keily pushed the girls in a specially-ordered stroller designed for triplets and smiled as people stared in delight at the girls beneath the canopy of the stroller.

Logan was proud of his girls, all of them.

Keily sidled up to him, in black flip flops, a sapphire blue sarong, and a matching bikini top that did little to hide her assets. He didn't mind a bit.

She'd started to wean the girls a couple of weeks ago but her bustline hadn't suffered for it. Neither had her waist, he noticed, she was almost back to her old size. Not that any of that really mattered, he'd loved her cushiony, he'd love her thinner too.

"I'm so glad you sprang this little trip on me last night." She sighed as she looked around. "It's so lovely here."

"It is, but not as lovely as you." He waggled his eyebrows at her and she laughed loudly, her eyes hidden behind dark sunglasses.

"That was just cheesy, Logan, but I'll take the compliment." She took a bottle of water from the compartment at the top of the stroller and drank. "Are you sure you should take your brace off?"

He looked down at the metal, cloth, and Velcro of the

soft cast he wore and frowned. He probably shouldn't, but as long as he was careful, maybe he wouldn't end up back in the ER. He'd been cleared for the trip when he reported no headaches or blurred vision and the only real display of the accident he'd managed to survive was the cast he had to wear. "Should be fine."

He hoped they weren't the famous last words of every male fool that ever lived.

They spent the first hour playing together in the water while Avery looked after the girls. He swam easily after her in the water, marveled at how well she swam, and when he started to get tired, he held her in his arms to kiss the salt from her lips. "I'm so glad we're here."

"I am too, Logan." She snuggled into his arms, her lips nuzzling at his neck.

Logan held her there and wanted to slip her bikini bottoms off but there were too many people around. Maybe he could get her in the pool later, once it was dark and Avery and the girls had gone to bed. Keily suddenly jolted and made a noise somewhere between a screech and a scream.

"I'm getting out, I don't know what that was that just brushed against my leg and I don't want to find out." She said as she swam away, fear evident in the way she didn't bother to look back.

He had to chuckle at her but stopped when he saw the telltale sign of a fin about thirty feet away. Not a good time to be in the water, he decided and followed her. He decided he wouldn't tell her what he'd seen, but he did keep his eyes open for that fin. It kept heading further out to sea and was gone by the time he walked out of the water behind Keily.

Avery sat on a huge blanket with the girls, two umbrellas spread out to keep the family in the shade. The babies were all asleep, seagulls swam on breezes in the sky, and the world was a peaceful place, despite the shark they'd just managed to calmly escape. Maybe they'd stay at the house the rest of the week, he decided, with a grim look back at the ocean before he sat down.

Families and friends filled the long expanse of sand and Logan decided it was the perfect time. Nobody was paying them any attention and the only people that mattered to him were right there. He didn't feel nervous, he knew in his heart what her answer would be, so after he dried his leg and put his cast back on, he dug out the ring box from the diaper bag he'd insisted on packing.

He tried to gather his thoughts, he'd had this all planned out, down to what he wanted to say, but now that the moment was at hand those words disappeared and he couldn't bring them back. A breeze blew over them, cooling their hot skin, but doing little for Logan's suddenly seized-up brain. He couldn't think of words, any words, to say. She was sitting there, not looking at him but at a family of seagulls fighting over something that had washed up on the beach.

"I think I'll go get a drink," Keily said out of the blue, her head tilted towards a little kiosk selling drinks and snacks.

"Keily...wait. Please?" Logan asked, still with the box in his hands. He felt the sand give another centimeter as he reached out to take her hand to stop her.

"What's up, Logan?" Keily asked and brushed hair out of her face, her sunglasses hiding her eyes from him. Then she glanced down at the box and he saw her eyebrows rise up over the sunglasses. It was a surprise then. "Logan?"

"Keily, I had a plan, a really good plan, and all these really great words I wanted to say. Stuff that would make it into movies, it was so good. But now that I'm here, looking at you, looking at the woman I want to spend the rest of my life with, my brain has just gone dead. I'm sorry the words aren't coming out better, but I want to tell you I love you."

He paused as she gasped, and a tear ran down from behind the huge sunglasses on her face. He didn't want her to cry, but if it was good crying that was fine. He rushed on to fill up the empty silence.

"I'm sorry I'm bungling this, but I do love you. Maybe the first time you hear those words from me shouldn't be the point where I'm asking you to be my wife, but that's just how it worked out. I love you. I love our girls. I want to spend the rest of my life with all of you, watching the girls grow up as we grow old together. Because I didn't know this, Keily, but I have a lot of love to give and the only people I want to give it to are you and our girls. So, will you marry me? Will you let me spend the rest of my life loving you?"

"Logan…" She started but then choked up. She'd been so afraid to let him back into her life that when she finally did, he thought she was past the bad times, past the things that could have torn them apart. Had he been wrong?

He frowned, his world about to collapse around him when she got up on her knees, pushed her glasses up on her head, and took his hand. This was it, he thought, afraid to meet her eyes, afraid to see her refusal there. He'd been so certain she'd say yes, but here he was, about to be thrown back into reality. Damn, he'd been a fool, he should have waited longer.

"Logan, I think for most of your life you haven't been loved. When I came to work for you, I don't think you *wanted* to be loved. You didn't know what it was, and it didn't fit into the goals you'd set in life. But I think you felt it, even when I didn't say it. Even when I didn't want to feel it, you felt it, despite our past, despite who I was when you came back into my life. The girls, they're our most precious gifts to each other, but you're mine,

Logan. Without you, I wouldn't have them, or be me, or know what real love was. I know two kinds of love now and yes, I want to spend the rest of my life with you, learning how love grows, changes, and what it's like to have that love for the rest of my life."

"Oh my." Avery sniffed behind Logan, but he didn't mind.

She'd said yes?

"Yes? You will marry me?" He whispered, too afraid she'd change her mind to speak louder.

"Yes, you goofy man, I'll marry you." Keily all but shouted and dozens of people around them started to clap and shout in happiness for them.

Logan looked around, surprised anyone had noticed their little moment, but pleased at the response. At *her* response. He pulled her into his arms, kissing her all over her face as she laughed at his response. *With* his response rather, he reminded himself.

"I hope it's the right size." He breathed as he took out the diamond ring, just the right size and shape for Keily's hand.

She was never ostentatious with jewelry and he'd chosen this one for a reason…it was a round, 2.5 gray carat diamond surrounded by smaller diamonds that matched the color of her eyes when she was most aroused. Only he would know that, though, he knew, and it pleased him that she'd wear his ring.

"It's beautiful, Logan, thank you." She held her left hand out, admiring the ring with Avery, just as one of the girls started to fuss and kick her legs.

People walked by and congratulated them in a mixture of Spanish and English. Logan said *gracias* to them all and meant it. This was one of the most important days of his life. He was pleased to have others to share it with.

"I'm still finishing school, though," Keily announced once she had Zoe changed and a bottle in her mouth. "I want to work for you."

"You can do whatever you like, Keily, as long as I get to do it with you," Logan answered and picked up Zinnia when she started to fuss.

"Hmm, I wasn't asking you, you know?" She narrowed her eyes at him but relaxed when he just smiled at her.

"I know, honey." He finally replied. "Thank you for accepting my rather pitiful attempt at proposing, by the way."

"I never in a million years expected it, Logan. You just aren't the type. Well, weren't the type, I should say. I guess you really have changed, and I love you for it."

"You wouldn't love me if I hadn't changed?" He asked, a little perplexed.

"I would, but you wouldn't have let yourself take a chance on it, so it's not me that would have changed the situation, it's you. I knew I loved you over a year ago. I've waited a long time for you to realize you loved me too." Keily sighed, her eyes stormy. "A lot happened, in both our pasts and lately with the babies. We had to change because of that, but the way we approached those things had to change. We've let it draw us together, instead of pushing us apart, and that's what matters. We're stronger together, and always will be."

"I love you, too, Keily." It felt nice to say it, and he didn't mind repeating it. He had a feeling he'd say it millions of times before his days were done.

"Good, because I need all the love I can get. Eventually, these three will leave us, and all I'll have is you. But that will be enough." She smiled a happy smile, full of joy and contentment.

"It will. And we can always adopt if we want more children. That's a promise." It was something that he'd thought about a few times now, but it was a decision for the future.

"Maybe when these three are older. Not before. No way." She chuckled and looked over at poor Avery, quietly wiping away the last of her happy tears. "Want to help me find a dress?"

"I'd love to, Keily. I really would." Avery sniffed and laughed at the same time.

This was going to be perfect, after all.

22

Keily

Once upon a time, Keily picked out the most expensive dress she could afford, invited everyone she knew, even in passing, to her wedding, and stressed herself out completely over everything being just right. In short, she'd been a bridezilla.

This time, she didn't care who was there, so long as her sister, niece, best friend, and Logan and their girls were there. She chose a dress that was comfortable in antique ivory lace, a beach dress the saleswoman called it, but that wasn't what Keily cared about. It wasn't virginal white, there was a slim ribbon belt at the waist, and it showed off enough cleavage to hold Logan's interest. There was a bit of girlishness in the flare at the bottom of the dress, but otherwise, it was suitable for a mother of three and a woman still young enough to want to feel pretty.

They didn't get married at a church, neither of them attended one, so they decided on a destination wedding and got married in Charleston, on the beach as it happened. Keily stood on the sand in bare feet, her toenails newly painted a bright, gaudy orange that she loved, and smiled up at her soon-to-be husband.

The girls were with Avery and Violet while Rosa served as her maid of honor and Logan stood with his second-in-command, Wally. He was the closest thing Logan had to a best friend. Keily noticed the way Wally kept eyeing Rosa, but she'd just broken up with her couple, she wasn't the least bit interested in a man. Or maybe she was… Keily had to wonder.

Alice served as their flower girl and ring bearer and that was the whole of their entourage. The only people that really mattered to any of them. Logan had invited Judith, but she'd declined because she had a cousin getting married the same day. That was fine, but they'd have liked the housekeeper, almost a mother to them both now, to be there.

Keily heard the words, repeated what she was supposed to, and stood there with a smile on her face, but she couldn't tell what was happening or if the ceremony was almost done. She was too caught up in the emotions flitting across Logan's face and the way his eyes kept getting sort of misty and red. He really did love her and it was heaven to know that for sure. She'd spent the majority of her life wanting to be loved, adored, but in the wrong ways, up until she met Logan. He'd changed everything, even her and now their girls were ten months old, and they were almost married.

Logan made his vows almost as robotically as Keily, but with a few more smiles and a charm that knocked her socks off. Her veil blew around in the breeze coming off the ocean and she pushed it away with annoyance. If that was the only thing that marred her day, however, she didn't care.

The officiant declared them man and wife, had them sign a paper, and was then off to go to another appointment. The few true friends and family they had rushed up to congratulate them and Keily hugged everybody, too caught up in the moment to hold back. With a baby on both hips and one on Logan's they left the beach to take pictures, and then went into the resort they'd booked into for the weekend.

"It all went so well," Violet exclaimed, her eyes full of happiness for her sister.

"I know. It's so much easier when you don't care who you're impressing or not impressing." Keily replied, and paused to let Rosa take Zoe from her hip as they walked into a restaurant for a private lunch reception. Although, with so few people, it might not really be a reception, Keily took comfort in knowing that these were the people that mattered, the only ones she and Logan wanted with them.

Logan had promised to take her on an adults-only honeymoon, back to their island escape later in the fall so this time with the family meant the world to Keily. The family she'd chosen for herself, not the one she was born with and forced to be around. Although, she refused even that now, she didn't have to be around people she didn't want to be near, and that was that.

"I imagine it is." Violet sighed and leaned over to her sister. "I'm getting married at Christmas."

"What?" Keily gasped and turned to stare at her sister. "You and the doctor?"

"He asked me just before I left to come here last night." Violet's cheeks turned red and she pulled Keily down into the chairs reserved for them. "He doesn't know it yet, but we're going to have a family of our own soon."

"Violet?" Keily gasped again, her eyes filled with joy. "Oh, my goodness! Come here."

Keily hugged her sister close and brushed at tears that spilled from her eyes. "I'm so happy for you."

"Not as happy as I am for you, Keily. And I mean that. I'm so happy for you."

"Thank you, sis." Keily squeezed a little tighter before she pulled away. "I'm glad you told me."

"Of course," Violet replied smartly with a teasing smile. "You're my big sister, who else would I tell first?"

"I don't know, but I'm glad it was me." Keily thought about how they'd lived separate lives, how they'd grown apart for a while, and was glad that they were back in each other's lives. Her sister was important to her and always would be now.

"Let's toast the happy couple, shall we?" Wally called out from Logan's left and stood to address the small crowd at the circular table covered in a white tablecloth. "I just want to say thank you to Logan for placing so much trust in me over the years, and for asking me to be his best man. I have to say, I never expected this, or for him to marry, but he couldn't have found a better wife than he's getting with Keily. And Keily, keep up whatever you're doing. I've never seen the man smile so much."

Logan groused at his best man but laughed. Keily leaned over to kiss away the moment of grumpiness from him, but his smile told her he wasn't really grumpy anyway. Once they'd eaten, Avery and Violet took the girls up to the suite Logan had rented and got them down for the night. Violet said she might come down later, but Keily had seen the tired tilt to her eyes and had a feeling she was snoring away in her own suite.

Keily had to stop breastfeeding quite early on because she wasn't making enough milk for all three babies, a product of the hysterectomy, her doctor told her. That and it was hard to keep three babies fed. They were on solid food now and not so dependent on her 24 hours a day. Which meant she could have a drink with her new husband and their friends, and they went down to the bar around 8 that evening. She wore a beach-ready simple black slouchy dress, still her favorite style, and a pair of strappy heels. Logan had on a pair of dark blue jeans with a black t-shirt that showed off just how in shape he was.

She knew exactly how in shape he was and planned to explore that body a little more later that evening. For now, she sipped at a gin and tonic and talked with Rosa.

"I can't believe they didn't want to come to the wedding," Keily said and glared at nothing in particular. "Or that they wanted you to not come."

"I don't know, something's going on there. They were starting to get really controlling and I'm not big on that. It's a reason I got divorced, you know? I wasn't about to let people I can't even marry do that." Rosa brushed it all off, but Keily knew she'd invested a lot of hopes and emotions into the unconventional relation-ship. "Maybe it's for the best. I don't think it was going to go much further anyway. Neither were ready to admit to their family that we were together, that I wasn't the best friend that just hung around a lot."

"I can understand fearing judgment, but maybe it's

best if you walk away. You're past the caring about judgment phase. If they aren't, then it won't work." Keily answered her friend with a pert nod. "No more fear."

She held up her glass and Rosa clinked her glass of wine to Keily's glass. "No more fear. And maybe some of whoever that guy is."

"Oh, you mean Wally?" Keily giggled and glanced over at her husband and his best man. "He is rather hot."

"Even if he does have an old-fashioned name."

"We can't help what our parents name us." Keily reminded her snickering friend. "Poor Logan was strapped with Eugene, remember?"

"I can't believe they did that to him," Rosa said, and Keily knew she meant more than the name. Logan had given Keily permission to explain a little about his life and the reason his parents weren't coming to the wedding was at the top of that list.

"I guess we aren't all meant to be parents. It seems his are getting divorced, at last." Keily revealed with lifted eyebrows. "He only found that out because his dad needed Logan's signature to turn over the house. Seems his dad has decided he wants to spend his golden years with his boyfriend."

"I see," Rosa said with a few rapid blinks. "That might explain things a little."

"Yes, it's hard to love someone when you don't love yourself." Keily picked up her glass and had a sip. "I'm going to go snag my husband for a dance, why don't you ask Wally, and you two join us?"

"I think I will. I'm not scared. Even if he is over six feet tall with the most gorgeous face I've ever seen." Rosa giggled in a rather girlish way and that set Keily off.

The giggles subsided once they joined the men standing at the bar for some reason. "What are you two doing over here on your own?"

"Just a minute of business babe, but it's done now," Logan answered his wife and leaned down to kiss her cheek. "Want to dance?"

"I'd love to." She twirled with his hand clasped in hers and pulled him towards the dance floor.

"Shall we join them?" She heard Wally ask Rosa and knew romance was in the air all around.

"Violet's getting married." She whispered to Logan who leaned back enough to stare down at her.

"Really?"

"Mmhmm. And she's pregnant." Keily's eyes were wide with excitement. "I'm going to be an aunt again. Apparently, daddy doesn't know yet, so that's just between us until she tells him."

"Our first secret as husband and wife. Ah, the life we're going to lead, Keily." Logan laughed and moved her around the floor expertly.

They danced to one of Logan's favorite songs, the

one about what love was that John Lennon wrote, the one that nearly broke him oh so long ago. Keily held onto him as the song touched off all the feels she could possibly feel and more. "I didn't know a song could be so perfect."

"I didn't either until I listened to it properly one day," Logan revealed and pulled her to him tightly, one last time, before they left the dancefloor and went back to the table where Rosa and Wally were chatting over new drinks. "I think love is in the air."

"Lust at least." Keily smothered a giggle and sat down. Rosa turned to her for a moment, her bottom lip between her teeth and her eyes scrunched up with excitement, before she turned back to Wally.

"I don't think we'll be missed if you want to head up to our suite." Logan leaned over to whisper into Keily's ear. Not many men could pull off a seductive whisper but most things Logan did could be considered seductive as far as Keily was concerned.

"Let me observe for a few more minutes, just because I'm nosy when it comes to Rosa, and then we'll go." As much as she loved her husband, she was consumed with curiosity about what was going on between Rosa and Wally.

They ended up staying for one more drink, and two more dances, before Logan growled in her ear that he'd had enough. "If you don't come with me now, I'm going to have to take you out somewhere dark and quiet and push that dress up around your hips, Keily. Do you want that?"

"Maybe I do, Logan," Keily whispered back, her gray eyes full of seduction. "Maybe I want a little bit of badness from you tonight?"

"Maybe I'll spank you if you keep that up." He growled again and grabbed at her bottom when he knew nobody was watching.

"Maybe I want you to." She growled back and reached up to kiss him quick and hot.

"We're going up, people, thanks for a beautiful day, but ours isn't over yet." Logan pronounced to their two friends suddenly and pulled Keily to him. "Ready, Mrs.?

"Ready, husband dear." She purred and waved at the couple at the table. "Night, night, don't let the bedbugs bite."

"I doubt I'll be sleeping if there's bedbugs, Keily. And if there is, I'm invading your room!" Rosa warned, but Keily had a feeling she wouldn't notice much of anything once Wally kissed her, which he clearly wanted to do if the way he looked at Rosa meant anything.

"They're definitely going to hook up." She said to Logan once they were alone in the elevator.

"Good for them, that's great." He muttered as he backed her up against the wall. They were on the fourth floor, so it wouldn't be a long ride, but long enough. "I don't give a fuck what they do, as long as it doesn't interrupt us."

"Hmm, but what about employee relations or whatever it's called." Keily pulled back away to tease him as she tried to remember the right word. "Fraternization. Isn't that a no-no in the employee handbook?"

"My lawyers put that in there to cover my ass. I don't care if those two fuck the night away, now shut up and kiss me or I'm going to die, Keily." He crushed his lips to hers in a fierce kiss that she didn't want to break. She wanted more of this slightly aggressive, just on the right side of bad Logan who was about to strip her down in an elevator. It was going to be one memorable night.

23

Keily

Logan managed to control himself until they got into the suite. He didn't manage to hold off until they got to the bed, however. She was in his arms and wrapped around him the second she walked through the door. He leaned into her until she leaned back against the door, ready to let him explore whatever he wanted to.

"I can't believe you agreed to marry me." He whispered as he trailed kisses down her neck.

"I can't believe we actually got married." She replied and hopped up to wrap her legs around his waist. "Are you going to take me out on that balcony so I can listen to the ocean as you fuck me?"

"If you like." He mumbled back, his tongue out to

taste her. "If I can manage to peel myself away from you."

"There is a rather sturdy-looking couch out there." She reminded him, but all he managed to do was murmur an agreement. He flexed his hands around her ass, and she slid down his body to stand on her feet, her face up to his, ready for whatever came next. His hands tugged at her dress to pull it off and she moved to allow him to pull it over her head.

"Hmm, lovely lace." He complimented her taste in pale pink panties with a matching bra. "But I really love the garter belt and stockings. It's just too bad they have to go."

"I'll wear them for you again some other time." She promised and tried not to whimper like a desperate teenager as he undid the bra and her nipples pressed into his chest. They were still so damn sensitive.

"Do you really want me to fuck you outside, Keily, can you wait that long?" Logan had her stripped bare for him now and his hand buried itself at the back of her head, using her hair as an anchor to pull. "Or do you want me to fuck you right here?"

"I want…" But he stopped her when he brought his face down to hers and kissed her so passionately that it took her breath away. When she had air to breathe again, a breath she stole as he unsealed his lips to slant his head, she moaned into his mouth. His hands were on her nipples, teasing the already tight peaks with such experienced hands that it nearly made her pass out. She inhaled his scent deep and forgot all about the couch outside.

"Come here." Logan guided her to the bedroom, so much closer than the balcony, and dropped his clothes as they went.

Her new husband guided her onto her back, his weight held away from her as his leg settled between her thighs. She gasped when his hands found the still soft flesh of her stomach, an area he knew she hated, but he adored. The scar on her abdomen, the marks left by her pregnancy showed how strong she was, what she'd been through, and he adored the place she hated the most about her body. He'd told her that, but she still worried he'd look at her one day with disgust.

"You're beautiful Keily, you always have been and you always will be. Nothing changes that. Every mark, every scar, only makes you more beautiful, darling." He said now, and she couldn't help but smile up at him.

"Only you could love me like that, Logan."

"Any man with sense in his head could love you like that, Keily, but they'll never get the chance, not as long as I have air in my lungs. I'm going to spend the rest of my life making sure you love me."

"I love you, too, Logan." She didn't have the perfect words, but those seemed to matter the most, so she repeated them. She pushed her arms around his neck as his fingers found the source of her hottest heat. She thought she said his name as his fingers teased at her with knowledge and just the right pressure.

He'd said he couldn't wait for her, but he turned that into a lie. His fingers continued to stroke at her, continued to spark pleasure that she couldn't ignore. Her fingers grasped at him, sliding across his chest, down further, to the very life and soul of him.

Keily cradled him in the heat in her hand for only a moment before he pulled away.

"I don't want to come yet, Keily. Let me hear you moan my name first."

She didn't want to, but she let him go, so that he could have his way. For now.

She contented herself with pressing kisses to his neck, to his shoulder, whatever she could touch as he moved lower, until he was completely out of reach.

His tongue and lips slowly slid down her body, over her breasts where they teased, over her abdomen where hot breath set her on fire, and further, down to the very core of her desire where his tongue took one long swipe to gather her taste, to make her back arch. "Logan."

He didn't reply verbally, not that she could hear, he just made her moan again by taking another long taste of her. The air rushed out of her lungs and her legs clamped around his head until he nudged them apart.

He needed air, she remembered for a second before she felt her legs trying to come together again. She forced them to stay apart, just enough that he could get air.

She loved him, but she was greedy when it came to pleasure. If he wanted her to get off first, then she'd make sure and take what he offered. There'd only be more to come anyway. A sultry smile stretched across her face as she ground her hips down, into his face, onto his tongue, her back an arch on the bed.

Pleasure blossomed every place his skin touched hers and it wasn't long before she forgot how to breathe altogether, held her breath, waiting for that pressure to explode in a ripple that would force air back into her lungs as her back bowed the other way. Her fingers clung to the quilt on the bed, grasped at him blindly, until that interminable moment when everything inside of her pulsed.

"Logan." She called out to him, wanting to tell him, bring him with her, but she couldn't say anything else. Words didn't come and thoughts fled into an oblivion of pleasure for what felt like days but might have only been a split second. She didn't know and she didn't care.

Logan's patience finally snapped, and she hadn't completely come down to earth when he rolled her over on the bed, pulled her up on her knees, and thrust into her smoothly and easily.

"Fuck, you feel so good." She heard him groan and knew she wasn't going to have to wait long.

His fingers dug into her hips, an exquisite pain that excited her more rather than put her off, but he didn't need to guide her, she was already thrusting back into him. Later she'd get him out on that balcony, and they'd make love, sweet, quiet love on the couch, but for now, they both needed sex. They'd done love the night before, tonight, it was raw pleasure they both needed.

"I thought about you all day, Keily, thought about this moment, when I'd have you as my wife for the first time." His words were short little gasps, timed to the thrust of their bodies.

Keily gasped in surprise when her walls pulsed around him suddenly, without warning and she wanted to pound the mattress in bliss.

"Damn, woman." He groaned, "I can't control myself when you do that."

"I can't help it." She gasped back. "It's your fault."

She felt his response inside of her, a pulse that made her growl with feminine power. There were a lot of ways that Logan made her feel like a woman in control. This was one of the best ways. He'd lost all control when he came, and she knew it.

She was still glowing with pleasure minutes later when he got up to get a bottle of water from the fridge. "You have a fine ass, Mr. Sinclair."

"As do you, Mrs. Sinclair."

"Aren't you glad I quit working for you now?" She asked, her hands behind her head, a sheet over her body.

"That might be the best day of my life, actually. Well, no, not really, but maybe."

"I'm sorry I lied about my resume." She admitted, at last, all these months later.

"I knew you did, babe, don't worry." He patted her hip and handed her the bottle, but she sat up to glare at him.

"You knew?"

"Of course, I did." He laughed and brushed it off. "It didn't matter. I have to admit, my intentions weren't exactly honorable at that point."

"I can't blame you." She mumbled and leaned back against his chest, her lips at his neck.

"I'm going to say this one last time, Keily, I don't blame you for what happened. For a time, I did, but what could you do back then? Joe and his friends were worse than pigs and would have attacked you if you'd tried. They had blood in their eyes, that night they attacked me."

"Joe's dad was pissed about him being drunk the night before. He'd yelled at all of them for puking in the pool."

"All of that because his dad yelled at him?"

"He was a child." Keily frowned. "Even when we'd

grown up, after we got married, he was a child. And yes, you're right. Let's not talk about him again."

Logan tucked her head into his neck, his fingers softly stroked at her hair. "We'll talk about whatever you want to talk about, Keily, whenever you need to. I just want you to stop feeling like that night was your fault, because it wasn't. There was nothing you could do and anything you tried might have made it worse. If they'd hurt you that night I'd have died."

"Do you remember when we were in the third grade and you brought me chocolates for Valentine's day?" The memory had resurfaced all of a sudden, and she turned to look at him. "I can't believe I forgot that."

"I remember, but only because you gave me a very chaste kiss on the cheek." Logan blushed, even now, at the memory.

"I wish things had turned out differently. I wish my mom hadn't subjected me to so much shit, but we made it, at last."

"We did, Keily. And I'm going to make sure you're happy for the rest of your life."

"Well, you did turn down my request for the balcony." She reminded him with a devilish grin. "And it is dark out there."

"I need more water first, woman. Don't want me to get a leg cramp, do you?" He teased but did take another drink of water.

"I only want you to be as happy as I am, Logan." She relented and moved to lean back against the headboard. "I really do."

"I love you for it, too."

"I love you, Logan." She responded quickly but meant it. "I know I've said it a thousand times, but I really didn't know what love was until you came along. I didn't care about anyone but myself. I was a horrid teenager and an even worse adult. You made me grow up, made me see that the reason I wasn't happy with the world had more to do with me than you."

"Well, you have your mother to thank for that." He tried to appease her and take the blame from her and she loved him for it every time he did it, but at the same time, she knew it wasn't right.

"I have to be accountable for who I was, Logan." She gave him a slight frown. "I could have chosen to be a different person when I left home."

"Yeah, but you were married to Joe before you knew it, and he was and is the world's biggest dick. Huge dick."

"He is, I know, but still, I was a huge bitch, so it was kind of equal there." Even if Joe deserved it. "Anyway, I just want you to know I realize that I was a spoiled little girl, and that the world doesn't revolve around me."

"I know you know that, but I hate to tell you this,

Keily. It does revolve around you now. My world does, anyway. Our daughters' worlds revolve around you."

"Well, you're our world. They adore you, you know? I love how happy they are when they see you."

"I do too. It's nice. I didn't know what I was missing out on and I'm glad I have them now. You and our girls, I think you all saved me from a life of bored loneliness. I wouldn't change our life for anything."

"You might change your mind when they're teenagers." She warned and tried not to shudder at the thought. "But that's a long way away."

"Yes, let's not rush puberty and boyfriends, and demands for prom dresses." He shuddered too and cringed. "We'll let them be little girls for as long as they want to be, thank you."

"I agree." She said and was about to roll over to tickle him, but her stomach growled with hunger.

"I'll see what time the restaurant closes, shall I?" Logan said with amusement.

"Sorry. I was still on cloud nine when we went to dinner and when you all ordered snacks earlier, I was too excited to eat. Is it too late?"

"Seems not." He answered after a glance over the menu by the phone. "What do you want?"

They dressed in robes while they waited for food and headed out to the balcony once it was delivered. The ocean rushed out there and she noticed a thoughtful look on Logan's face. "What's up?"

He put down his burger and looked over at her. "There was a shark in the water that day we were at the beach in Puerto Rico."

"Are you kidding me?" She stared at him, her eyes wide with shock. "Is that why you didn't want to go back to the beach?"

"It was. I didn't want to worry you, but it reminds me of what I have to lose if I'm not careful." He shrugged and picked his burger back up. "But don't worry, I'd have torn that shark apart with my bare hands and teeth if it came near you."

"I don't think I'll be going back in the water any time soon." She assured him and sank back, her belly as full as her heart now. "That'll be one worry off your mind."

"It will." His voice trailed off. "But how am I going to talk you out of this exhibitionism you're so enamored with?"

"You're not, and you know it." She got up from the table to walk over to him and straddle his lap. "In fact, you promised me a little bit of fun out here. I think it's time to collect."

"You might be right, Mrs. Sinclair." The burger dropped from his hands to cup her breasts. "And I'm going to love every minute of it."

"Me too." She started to say but it cut off in a gasp as his fingers and lips found her nipples.

Keily had changed a lot since Logan walked back into her life, but one thing would never change. She loved Logan with every fiber of her being and she'd prove it every day for the rest of her life. No matter how she changed, how much she grew up, or what kind of wisdom she gained, he was her husband now and she'd be his wife.

TWISTED INTENTION
~ A billionaire revenge romance series ~
Twisted Beauty
Twisted Love
Twisted Fate

Mafia's Obsession
~ A hot mafia romance series ~
Mafia's Dirty Secret
Mafia's Fake Bride
Mafia's Final Play

Screaming Demons
~ An MC romance series full of suspense ~
Rough Start
Rough Ride
Rough Choice
Rough Patch
Rough Return
Rough Road
Rough Trip
Rough Night
Rough Love

Standalone Contemporary Romance
Billionaire in Vegas
Billionaire Hunt

Billionaire's Game
Billionaire Retreat
Billionaire On Air
A Chance To Love
Somebody To Love
Not Mine To Love

Check out Summer's entire collection at
www.summercooper.com/books

ABOUT SUMMER COOPER

Thank you so much for reading. Without you, it wouldn't be possible for me to be a full-time author. I hope you enjoy reading my books as much as I do writing them.

Besides (obviously!) reading and writing, I also love cuddling my dogs, shouting at Alexa, being upside down (aka Yoga) and driving my family cray-cray!

Get in touch at
hello@summercooper.com
www.summercooper.com

facebook.com/summercooperauthor
instagram.com/summercooperauthor
goodreads.com/summercooper
bookbub.com/profile/summer-cooper

www.ingramcontent.com/pod-product-compliance
Lightning Source LLC
Chambersburg PA
CBHW051305210726
48287CB00002B/683